The Young Oxford

TRAIN STORIES

Dennis Hamley

OXFORD
UNIVERSITY PRESS

OXFORD

UNIVERSITY PRESS

Great Clarendon Street, Oxford OX2 6DP

Oxford University Press is a department of the University of Oxford.
It furthers the University's objective of excellence in research, scholarship,
and education by publishing worldwide in

Oxford New York

Athens Auckland Bangkok Bogotá Buenos Aires Calcutta
Cape Town Chennai Dar es Salaam Delhi Florence Hong Kong Istanbul
Karachi Kuala Lumpur Madrid Melbourne Mexico City Mumbai
Nairobi Paris São Paulo Shanghai Singapore Taipei Tokyo Toronto Warsaw

and associated companies in Berlin Ibadan

Oxford is a registered trade mark of Oxford University Press
in the UK and in certain other countries

British Library Cataloguing in Publication Data available

ISBN 0 19 278170 7 (hardback)

ISBN 0 19 278171 5 (paperback)

1 3 5 7 9 10 8 6 4 2

Typeset by AFS Image Setters Ltd, Glasgow

Printed in Great Britain
by Biddles Ltd, Guildford and King's Lynn

For my grandson Joe,
in the hope that both trains and stories
will mean as much to him
as they have to me.

Contents

Introduction

Why trains? Dirty old things, slow, noisy, crowded, late. Yes, I know. But they're also wonderful chariots, once really chariots of fire, still chariots of romance, crossing whole countries, whole continents, where adventures can always happen.

From the moment these great snorting, smoking monsters appeared in countryside quiet for centuries, stories have been written and told about them. Stories of danger and menace, stories of happiness and laughter. Love stories, spy stories, murder stories, and, most of all—ghost stories. For when the great express looms up out of the night after its long journey, you never know who—or what—is travelling on it.

I asked some top children's authors to write about what trains conjured up for them and scoured books to find stories already written. You'll stop an accident at the very dawn of railways, you'll meet unexpected passengers on Eurostar and the Californian Zephyr, you'll be the fireman on a steam engine a hundred years ago. In Australia, you'll see a disaster magically averted and then drive an old engine along forbidden tracks, you'll find something dangerous in an Indian tunnel before the Night Mail comes through. You'll take mysterious journeys on strange, unearthly trains.

And much, much more. All these stories celebrate the fascination of trains and railways. If, after reading them, you look at the next train you go on with new eyes, I'll be well pleased—and even more if you look really hard and say, 'There's a story here.'

I want to thank three people who gave huge advice and help in making this collection: Chris Smith of *The School Librarian*, my good friend Dennis Pepper, best of all anthology compilers, and Ron Heapy, doyen of children's editors.

Dennis Hamley

Mystery Train

DAVID BELBIN

'It's like a plane!' Rick Brown said, as he stepped inside the superliner.

'That's right,' Dad said. 'Only the seats have more leg-room.'

Excited, Rick explored the smart carriage. It had two levels, like the double-decker buses back home in London.

Rick's family had spent two and a half weeks cooped up in a car. He, his older sister, Jodie, and Mum and Dad had enjoyed exploring California. They'd also got on each other's nerves. Now they were on board the California Zephyr from Sacramento to Chicago. It was the last leg of their holiday. By unspoken agreement, they left each other alone. Mum had her newspaper, Jodie her puzzle magazine, and Rick his hand-held computer. Dad went off to the lounge car.

Rick looked at Mum's paper. The headline was about some singer who died ages ago. Lots of people thought he wasn't really dead. So they were going to dig up his coffin and make sure that the body inside really was him. Gruesome.

On the tannoy, the conductor gave out a long list of instructions.

'Federal Law requires you to wear footwear at all times.'

'Jodie, put your shoes back on,' Mum said.

'Why?'

'I don't know. There must be a good reason.'

Sulking, his sister did as she was told. The train started off.

'I'm going to take a look in the observation car,' Rick told Mum.

'All right, but don't disturb your father if he's there. He needs to unwind.'

Stepping between carriages, Rick realized why you had to keep your shoes on. The carriages moved about. Feet could get trapped in the gaps between them.

The track curved and he could see the rest of the train. Behind his carriage were three similar ones, coaches full of seats. Behind them were the freight carriages. Rick couldn't tell how many of them there were. In front of him was the lounge car, then four sleeping cars. Beyond those were the two engines which pulled the train along.

The observation deck was on the upper level of the lounge car. Windows went nearly all the way to the top. The observation deck had posh seats which swivelled around. Rick looked for his father on one of them but he wasn't there.

While he was here, Rick decided, he might as well visit one of the sleeping cars. He'd have liked to go in one of these, but Dad said they were too pricey—three times as much as sitting in coach. Rick looked around. The small cabins seemed unoccupied. Maybe people

would be joining the train later in the journey. Rick took the stairs down to the lower level.

There, with his back to Rick, was the attendant. Rick could see the black man leaning through a doorway, talking to somebody.

'So you won't be disturbed, sir,' he was saying.

'I'm sure you'll do a fine job, Waldo,' a deep voice replied.

Rick, not sure if he was allowed to be on this carriage, hurried back to the lounge car. There, on the lower level, was his father, drinking a beer at the bar.

They ate lunch between Colfax and Lake Tahoe. The train climbed into the Sierra mountain range, which was the most awesome sight Rick had ever seen. As Rick stared, Dad talked about trains.

'The USA used to have hundreds of train companies. Rich people had their own private carriages. Now they have limousines instead. The automobile killed off the railways.'

Mum started talking about the newspaper article she'd been reading, the one about the dead singer.

'There's all sorts of things that don't add up. His middle name was spelt wrong on his gravestone. There was no inquest, no photographs of the death scene. And nobody ever claimed on his life insurance policy.'

'Maybe his relatives had enough money already,' Dad said. 'Next you'll be telling me that you believe those stories about people seeing him shopping in supermarkets. Can we change the subject?'

He glanced in Rick's direction, as if to indicate that Rick was too young to hear such unsavoury stuff. But Rick could read. He had seen the newspaper earlier.

And he'd read several stories where people faked their own death.

Later, Rick picked up Mum's paper and read the piece about the singer. The exhumation would take place on Wednesday, the day they got to Chicago. Earlier, Mum had missed one thing out. On the singer's death certificate, he was listed as weighing 170 pounds. Yet, only days before, the singer was known to weigh 250 pounds. Was it a mistake? Or was there a different body in the coffin?

The train rolled through the spectacular mountains. You were only meant to stay in the observation car for fifteen minutes at a time. However, there weren't many people on the train, so Rick kept going back.

By nightfall, they were travelling through the Nevada desert. After Elko, most people went to sleep. The seats folded out and were quite comfortable. Still, Rick couldn't get off. He got up to use the toilet, then decided, while he was up, to take a last look out from the observation car.

It was a moonlit night. The desert seemed to sparkle. Rick found it restful to look at. Within minutes, he'd dozed off.

He woke again with a jolt. For a moment, he thought that they'd arrived in Salt Lake City. Then he looked at his watch. Four in the morning. He ought to return to his seat. If Mum or Dad woke, they'd worry about him. He hurried back.

Still half asleep, he must have taken a wrong turn, for there were no seats in the carriage he stepped onto. It was dark and eerie. Rick was about to go back the way he had come. Then he saw light, seeping through the door at the other end of the corridor. He heard singing.

Without really knowing why, Rick walked down the

corridor. For the first time, he noticed that the door to the room at the end had no number. Rick listened to the soft, sweet voice coming from inside. It wasn't a recording. There were no backing instruments, just the voice, singing softly. Rick listened, caught up in the music. Then, behind him, he heard a door open, followed by a squeaking sound.

Should he be there? Rick didn't belong on this carriage. Quickly, he stepped back into the empty baggage area. He hid just in time. The squeaking sound was the shoes of the attendant he'd seen earlier. Waldo knocked on the numberless door.

'I have your coffee and doughnuts, sir.'

'Thanks, Waldo. Bring them in.'

Once the attendant was inside, Rick hurried upstairs. The moon had gone in. Outside was pitch black. All Rick could see was the light cast by the train. No. There was something else. Rick paused to look. Over on the left, he could make out artificial light and large white mounds, like little mountains made of clouds.

'Shouldn't you be in your seat, son?' It was Waldo, the attendant from the other carriage. His voice was kind.

'What are those?' Rick asked, pointing.

'Why, those are salt mounds. That over there is the Salt Lake, where most of the salt in the country comes from. They take it out of the lake, twenty-four hours a day. Now, get going before your mummy and daddy worry about you.'

'Top of the morning, America,' said the voice over the tannoy. 'This is your steward speaking. I have freshly brewed coffee here to help you start your day the right way.'

Dad rubbed his eyes, then headed to the lounge car for coffee. Soon, they were at Grand Junction. People rushed onto the platform, looking to buy newspapers and food from any stall that happened to be open. Dad, Mum, and Rick went to the restaurant car for breakfast. Jodie, meanwhile, hurried onto the platform to get a magazine. Mum gave her fifty cents to pick her up a copy of *USA Today*, which Jodie came back with ten minutes later.

'Look at this leader article,' Mum said, as Rick tucked into pancakes with bacon, ice-cream, and Maple syrup. 'It says *The King is dead and tomorrow they prove it. Wednesday, the conspiracy theorists will be silenced. Either that, or America is in for its biggest shock since the attack on Pearl Harbor.*'

'It's not as important as all that,' Dad said. 'He was just a singer.'

'Of course he's important,' Mum said. Then she started to go on about how he'd been the first white rock'n'roll singer and influenced all sorts of people. He'd died when she was very young but still she loved his music. 'It was fame that he couldn't stand,' Mum said. 'Towards the end of his life, in Memphis, he would only go out late at night, in disguise. Sometimes, he even got his bodyguards to hide him in the boot of his car, so that he wouldn't be seen by fans at the gate.'

'A lot of people would kill to have the problems he had,' Dad commented.

'How old would he be?' Jodie asked. 'I mean, if he was still alive?'

'Not that old,' Mum said. 'Somewhere in his sixties, I think.'

That seemed pretty old to Rick. He wasn't much interested in music, but glanced over Mum's shoulder at the story about the singer. Surely it would be great

if everybody loved you, wanted to be seen with you. Why would you need to hide, to disguise yourself? It couldn't hurt to sign a few autographs.

The Zephyr zigzagged through the Rockies. Rick wanted to catch up on his sleep, but there was always loads to see. Now and then, curious about the room with no number, he took a look in the sleeping car. The numberless door was always closed. He checked the Amtrak brochure, which had diagrams showing all the carriages. There wasn't meant to be a compartment there, only storage. But the first sleeping car looked older than the others beyond it. Also, it had a golden eagle embossed on one of its outer doors. None of the other cars had one.

They were still running late. As night began, the attendant came round the carriage, closing all the windows. Rick asked why.

'Diesel fumes. You'll see in a few minutes.'

'The Moffat tunnel's coming up,' Dad explained.

Through the windows, Dad pointed out the old railway lines, the ones that the pioneers had ridden on as they returned from the gold rush. Then, suddenly, they were in the tunnel. For six miles, the train travelled through pitch black. When it came out at the other end, the train began a rapid descent. It was like being on a rollercoaster, only this was much more than a theme park ride. The train travelled in vast curves, dropping through the mountains with massive switchbacks.

It was nightfall when they left Denver, and the journey was more than half done. Rick, suddenly exhausted, fell asleep soon after dinner. The Zephyr was travelling through prairie. It was a cloudy night. There was little to see. Rick slept heavily.

When he woke it was, once again, early in the morning. Rick needed the toilet. On the way, he took a peek through the windows. He couldn't make much out. Maybe he should go up to the observation deck again.

It was four, the time he'd woken the night before. There was nothing to see from the observation deck, but, below, he could hear Waldo, working. The attendant was in the bar, preparing a snack for the stranger in the sleeping car.

Rick hurried to the car ahead of Waldo. Once again, he hid in the baggage area. The room without a number was silent. Rick heard the squeaking of the trolley, then watched as Waldo knocked on the door. Slowly, it opened.

'I've brought your burgers and soda, sir, as requested.'

'You're a good man, Waldo.'

Rick tried to get a glance at the man as Waldo took the snack in, but saw nothing. A moment later, as Waldo left, Rick seized his chance. The door to the compartment was not yet fully closed. He put his foot out to stop it shutting. He only wanted a look, that was all. He wanted to test the suspicion he'd had since he heard the man singing to himself the night before. At the far end of the corridor, Waldo shut the carriage door behind him.

'Who's there?' The voice was gentle, warm.

'Excuse me.' Rick pushed the door open. The man was sitting in shadow. Rick could see his silhouette against the window. 'I was curious,' Rick said.

'Couldn't sleep, huh? You might as well come in.

Want one of my burgers? There's more here than I need.'

The smell was making Rick hungry. As he wolfed down the greasy bun, the man asked Rick his name and where he was from. Rick told him.

'I'd like to visit your country,' the man commented. 'I changed planes there once, but didn't get to see a thing. You still have a lot of trains there, I hear.'

'Not as many as there used to be,' Rick replied. Then he summoned up the courage to ask the questions that were on his mind.

'What is this compartment? I looked in the brochure, and there's meant to be a storage area here.'

'Not all trains are the same,' the man said. 'This is a private carriage. It belongs to me.'

'Is that why there's an eagle on one of the doors?'

'Yes. This car looks like all the others, but nobody else ever travels on it. Not many people ever use the sleeping cars, anyway. Very few people use trains in America. They're a good place for a man to get lost in.'

'What's your name?' Rick asked.

'I think you know that already.'

The man leant forward so that Rick could half see his face. It was gaunt and lined. Still, the man was handsome, and strangely familiar.

'Do you believe in ghosts?' the man asked.

Rick shook his head.

'Me neither. But some people choose to become a kind of ghost. These ghosts aren't spirits. They're living people who walk the earth in secret. We watch the world, but we don't take part in it any more. That's what I am. A ghost.'

'But why?' Rick asked. 'Why did . . . '

The man wasn't listening. He was staring out of the window, burger uneaten by his side. Somehow, Rick

knew that he wouldn't get an answer. Quietly, the man
began to sing. He sang about a long black train, coming
right down the line. The train had taken his baby away,
but she was coming back. The man swore that he
would never let the train take her away again.

He wasn't singing about this train. The one in the
song was sixteen coaches long. Was it a real train, or
just a song? Rick knew better than to ask. As the song
ended, the singer gave a high pitched yelp, almost like
a train whistle. Then he sang another song. Then
another. Rick listened to the man singing for a long
time.

Suddenly, the light in the corridor outside came on
and the tannoy spoke.

'Good morning, America. It's 6 a.m. We'll be in
Lincoln in a few minutes.'

'You better get going,' the man said.

Rick hurried to the door. Then he remembered
something.

'You ought to know,' he said. 'I read it in the
papers. Today, they're going to . . . '

'I know,' the man told him. 'Don't worry yourself. I
have friends who help me. Off you go now.'

The Zephyr was nearly four hours late getting into
Grand Union Station, Chicago.

'Your bags will be ready in a couple of minutes,' the
attendant from Rick's carriage said, putting out the step
for them to get off.

As they walked to the baggage reclaim area, Rick
looked ahead. The sleeping cars and engines were
already being shunted away. There was no sign of the
man from the numberless compartment.

'Excuse me,' Rick said to the attendant. 'That

carriage with the golden eagle on the door—who does it belong to?'

'What carriage?' the man replied. Rick tried to point but it was already out of sight.

'The one that Waldo works on,' he said.

'Ain't nobody called Waldo works on the Zephyr.'

As the Browns left the station building, a tannoy announced that the train to Memphis was about to leave. Anybody not travelling on it should get off now. Mum stopped to buy an evening paper. Rick hurried over to get a look at the Memphis train. It was much shorter than the Zephyr. Rick could see a sleeping car being hooked up to it, right behind the engine. If he screwed his eyes up, he could make out something embossed on one of the doors. An American eagle.

Mum was strangely quiet as she returned.

'It was him in the coffin,' she whispered to Dad. 'He was there all along.'

She was upset, Rick saw, and she didn't need to be. But he was only a kid. There was nothing he could tell her which she would believe, or understand. As they left the building, the Memphis train began to roll down the line. Rick heard what sounded like a high pitched whistle, or a yelp. It sounded like freedom.

Don't Let Go

MARILYN WATTS

Robert was terrified of trains. Always had been, ever since he could remember. Ever since he was a baby.

He wasn't a baby now, of course. He was in the football team at school, and one of the tallest boys in his class. He could even cope with Joe Edwards and his gang on a good day. There wasn't much that bothered him.

Except his secret. His fear. Only one other person knew. One particular other person.

Long ago, when Robert was a baby, his Aunt Katrina had given him a toy. A train. Soft and squishy, yellow and green. It lay with him in his cot, solid against the white sheet and the light bars.

When he was one, Uncle Andrew bought him a book. *Thomas the Tank Engine*, blue and black. Pages made of board for chewing on. Thick pages, curved at the edge so they wouldn't hurt your fingers. A button in the top corner. When you pressed it, it made a noise like a train. On and on the sound went, even though you didn't touch it any more. Baby Robbie was

fascinated. He could make the noise happen. Clever. A wonderful, powerful feeling. Clever hands. Press the button. Chuff, chuff chuff, chuff chuff-chuff-chuff. Press the button. Chuff, chuff chuff, chuff chuff-chuff-chuff . . .

When Robert was two, it started. The secret, and the fear.

Mum and Dad took him to the station. For a treat, they said. They didn't use trains as a family—the car was so much more convenient. But they took him to the station, to watch the trains coming in and out. 'Robert likes trains,' they said. 'All those Thomas books.'

They took Lucy too. Lucy was Robert's big sister, six years older. Too big, really. She had wide blue eyes and light, fluffy hair. She was very pretty. Lucy meant light, shining like St Lucia. Lucy wasn't like light, and she wasn't at all a saint. When she looked at Robert her blue eyes narrowed. Robert knew this, but none of the grown-ups noticed. Lucy's mouth was too thin. She used to creep into his room, alone, and poke him through the bars of the cot. Then she would pull his train back out through the bars and hurl it to the floor.

'Oh, not again,' his parents would say, smiling. 'You're always throwing your toys out, aren't you, Robbie?'

Now, at the station, they walked up the steps on to the platform. The steps were high, and difficult for two-year-old Robert to climb. The station itself was busy, big, and noisy. A train stood alongside, a few people climbing in. Robert looked at them through the long windows. The curving glass stretched and twisted the reflections. The train was dark and dirty. The people looked tired. Another train chuntered through on the other platform. 'Look,' said his parents, spinning him around. 'Look, Robert. There's another one.'

Robert looked. These trains weren't like Thomas. Thomas was round and soft, with a clean white face and smiley eyes.

The first train swished shut its doors, groaned, and stretched itself off along the track. Robert leaned over to watch it go. Lucy's hand was hard on his back, pushing him.

'Careful, Robert.' His mother's hand tightened on his. Lucy's fingers were dug into his coat. Still a threat.

And then, 'Listen,' Lucy whispered. 'It's coming.'

At first Robert could hear nothing. Then a slight humming sound, far off. It grew, mixed with a high whine. There was pressure on the small of his back, but his mother pulled him towards her, away from the edge. Lucy's fingers lost their grip.

A monster screamed through in front of him, blocking out the light, blocking out the station. Suddenly there was nothing except noise, a huge noise of screeching and metal and a smell which caught in his throat and made his eyes water. And then he was dragged, spinning, falling into blackness.

He blinked his eyes. It was dark, cold in front of his face. His body was pushed up against something cold and hard. He blinked. Metal touched his cheek, his eyelashes flicked against it. Whatever it was, it wasn't moving. He flicked his eyelashes again. Groaned.

'Keep holding on.' Lucy's voice hissed in his ear like wheels on the track. 'Don't let go. If you let go, the wind will blow you away. That's what happens to little children. Careful, there's another fast train coming, another one that won't slow down. You're too small and light, you know that? If you let go, it'll take you away.'

That noise again. Roaring. Screaming.

Robert held on for dear life. The world spun again.

Then someone else was there. His mother, trying to prise his fingers off the grey metal post. 'Robbie,' she asked. 'Hey, Robbie. Whatever's the matter?'

But he couldn't answer, of course, and he wouldn't let go. Couldn't. Dare not. His mother forced his fingers open and he clung on to her coat instead, sobbing.

'Robbie, darling. What is it?'

He couldn't tell her. What was the point? They had brought him to this place which was so dangerous. Lucy knew all about it. They must have brought her too, when she was little? Why?

The train would have taken him. Blown him away with the noise and the rushing wind. Lucy was big and knew all kinds of things. She must be right. But why did his parents take him somewhere that they could lose him? It was too big an idea. Robert shook his head to shake it away, and sobbed.

'Not a great success, the station outing,' his parents said wryly. They suggested another visit, but Robert just cried. 'OK,' they said. 'We'll stick to Thomas until you're older.'

At home, Lucy showed him a picture in her book. A train station. One big dark train threatening at the platform. Another sneaking up the track. 'If you're naughty, they'll take you again.' Robert looked at her, eyes wide. 'They took me three times,' she assured him. 'But I held on tight every time. Then I stopped being naughty. Give me your biscuit. If you don't, I'll tell Mum you're eating my biscuit. That's naughty . . . '

He gave her the biscuit. Many biscuits.

'Such good children,' people would say. 'You know, I don't think I've ever heard them argue.'

'Oh they do,' said Mum. But she sounded pleased.

'Not very often, though. They always seem to sort it out between themselves, don't you?'

Lucy smiled. Robert nodded. Yes, it was all sorted out between themselves.

And it stayed sorted, while time chuffed along and Robert learnt all kinds of things. He learnt that he would never catch up with Lucy. She knew so much already. And she could run faster than he could, ride a bike without stabilizers, make shapes into reading. While Robert tried to swim without armbands, Lucy was up there learning to dive. She stood on the side of the pool, feet clamped to the edge. Robert longed to push her in, send her crashing into the water. His hand wavered at her back. Send her flying, whisked up through the air. But he never dared. Not then.

There were many things he never dared. Mum and Dad used to try to get him to do things. 'Come on, Robert,' they'd say. 'It won't hurt you. It's all right.' But he would simply catch Lucy's eye and know. It wasn't safe. You could never be sure where the danger would come from, hurtling through without stopping. So many things for Lucy to warn him about.

Years of time had run through when, finally, he had to go to the station again. They all went, to meet his aunt and uncle off the train. His parents laughed as they made their way up the dark staircase towards the platform. 'Do you remember the first time we brought you here, Robert?'

'I remember,' said Lucy, smugly. 'He *screamed*.'

'It was a long time ago,' his mother said, quickly.

The staircase was very steep, and at the top they stood on an island in the middle of the tracks. Gorges on each side where the platform fell away and the harsh rails ran. Robert held on to the handrail, and only let go when his father, exasperated, insisted he come away from the stairs. He sidled along the platform, holding on to a pillar here, a sign there. He wanted to sit in the waiting room, but a note on the door said *Out of Order*. How could a room be Out of Order? They sat on the platform instead, on a long bench that luckily was screwed down, and Robert gripped the seat with his hands. His knuckles showed white. Lucy saw this, of course.

'Hold tight!' she whispered. 'Don't let go. I can hear a train coming.'

Robert was older now, but not old enough. Part of his brain told him not to believe her, that it couldn't be true, but the rest of him wouldn't listen. His mouth went dry, a hammer pounded in his head, and his heart raced like the train that thundered though the station making the metal shake and the pieces of paper on the platform fly up in his face to mock him.

Lucy jumped to her feet, dragged at his coat.

'Come on, Robert,' she said. 'It'll be their train soon. Let's go and look for it.'

'Careful,' said their father. 'Don't go near the edge.'

'We won't.' Lucy's eyes became bigger and bluer. 'Of course we won't. We'll just go a bit nearer the end of the platform.' And beneath it she muttered, 'I dare you.'

Robert watched her, mouth shut tight.

'I dare you,' she muttered.

He didn't move.

'Coward,' she said. 'I'm going to tell them at school.'

Robert didn't say a word. Couldn't. His fingers uncurled from the bench seat and crunched up again in his palms. Nails digging into his hands, elbows clenched to his sides, body angled away from that terrible edge of platform and those terrible screaming

trains. But he followed her along to where the express trains whistled down.

Followed her.

She turned to him, sneering. 'Bet you daren't stay there when the next train comes.' A smile, lip curled. 'Bet you hold on to something again, don't you, baby. Scaredy cat.'

Pink lips, laughing at him. Blue eyes, scornful. Hands on hips, turning away from him dismissively.

The tearing, screaming monster coming from behind them, nearer and nearer. So fast. Track jolting and squealing, shuddering and screeching. A rush of air. Hands uncurled, arms outstretched, two quick paces. Louder and louder. Not holding on to anything, but reaching for someone and pushing, quick and hard.

Screaming.

Unbelievable, they said afterwards. A freak accident. Whatever could have happened?

The girl lost her balance or something. The train must have set up some strange turbulence, like a wind tunnel or a tornado. They'd have to check the station design at that part of the platform, make sure it can't happen again. Do some tests. Incredible. The driver wasn't going any faster than usual. Not sure what happened.

There was no agreement on why, but everyone knew what had happened. The express train, roaring through the station. Not stopping, not letting up speed. And a girl pulled off her feet by the force of it, blown away by the wind of the train as it raced through. Her little brother was there—but he wasn't affected. Tried to grab her or something, but couldn't.

Robert saw her lift up, whirl through the air. It was like throwing one of her dolls. He watched her crash to the wall, drowned by the noise of the train, but he

knew she would have been screaming. He looked at his hands. Curled his fingers. He must be very strong. Powerful. He could make things happen. The drama went on without him. People rushing, grabbing him away from the platform. His mother crying. Silence where Lucy's hissing voice had been. Robert standing on the platform, not holding on. Clever. Looking on while they took her away. Clever hands.

It was quieter in the hospital. Calm and still. People didn't rush around, but walked efficiently on moulded heels. Lucy lay in the white bed. Lucy, light. Around Lucy's bed it was very quiet. They came to visit. Often.

Robert sat by her bed. He could hear his mother's voice outside the curtains. 'He's brought that baby book again,' she said. 'It's as if he's regressing as well. I can't cope with two of them . . . '

'We'll see.' That was his father's voice. 'He's had a shock. Let him act like a little kid if he wants to, for a while. Until he gets over it.'

'Gets over it!'

'Oh, you know what I mean. As much as anyone can get over it. Seeing that happen to his sister—must have been such a shock . . . '

Lucy's eyes were shut. Wide blue eyes shut tight. Her fluffy hair was trapped in the thick bandage that covered her head. On the white blanket, her hand lay still. Bright Lucia.

In the chair, Robert had his book with him. Thick pages, curved at the edge so they wouldn't hurt your fingers. A button in the top corner. When you pressed it, it made a noise like a train. On and on the sound went, even though you didn't touch it any more. Chuff, chuff chuff, chuff chuff-chuff-chuff.

Lucy opened her eyes at the sound. Blue eyes,

stretched so very wide. Her fingers twitched on the blanket.

Robert smiled. He could make the noise happen. Clever. A wonderful, powerful feeling. Clever hands. Press the button. Chuff, chuff chuff, chuff chuff-chuff-chuff. Press the button. Chuff, chuff chuff, chuff chuff-chuff-chuff . . .

The Tunnel

RUSKIN BOND

It was almost noon, and the jungle was very still, very silent. Heat waves shimmered along the railway embankment where it cut a path through the tall evergreen trees. The railway lines were two straight black serpents disappearing into the tunnel in the hillside.

Ranji stood near the cutting, waiting for the mid-day train. It wasn't a station and he wasn't catching a train. He was waiting so he could watch the steam-engine come roaring out of the tunnel.

He had cycled out of town and taken the jungle path until he had come to a small village. He had left the cycle there, and walked over a low, scrub covered hill and down to the tunnel exit.

Now he looked up. He had heard, in the distance, the shrill whistle of the engine. He couldn't see anything, because the train was approaching from the other side of the hill; but presently a sound like distant thunder came from the tunnel, and he knew the train was coming through.

A second or two later the steam-engine shot out of the tunnel, snorting and puffing like some green, black and gold dragon, some beautiful monster out of Ranji's dreams. Showering sparks right and left, it roared a challenge to the jungle.

Instinctively Ranji stepped back a few paces. Waves of hot steam struck him in the face. Even the trees seemed to flinch from the noise and heat. And then the train had gone, leaving only a plume of smoke to drift lazily over the tall *shisham* trees.

The jungle was still again. No one moved.

Ranji turned from watching the drifting smoke and began walking along the embankment towards the tunnel. It grew darker the further he walked, and when he had gone about twenty yards it became pitch black. He had to turn and look back at the opening to make sure that there was a speck of daylight in the distance.

Ahead of him, the tunnel's other opening was also a small round circle of light.

The walls of the tunnel were damp and sticky. A bat flew past. A lizard scuttled between the lines. Coming straight from the darkness into the light, Ranji was dazzled by the sudden glare. He put a hand up to shade his eyes and looked up at the scrub-covered hillside, and he thought he saw something moving between the trees.

It was just a flash of gold and black, and a long swishing tail. It was there between the trees for a second or two, and then it was gone.

About fifty feet from the entrance to the tunnel stood the watchman's hut. Marigolds grew in front of the hut, and at the back there was a small vegetable patch.

It was the watchman's duty to inspect the tunnel and keep it clear of obstacles.

Every day, before the train came through, he would walk the length of the tunnel. If all was well, he would return to his hut and take a nap. If something was wrong, he would walk back up the line and wave a red flag and the engine-driver would slow down.

At night, the watchman lit an oil-lamp and made a similar inspection. If there was any danger to the train, he'd go back up the line and wave his lamp to the approaching engine. If all was well, he'd hang his lamp at the door of his hut and go to sleep.

He was just settling down on his cot for an afternoon nap when he saw the boy come out of the tunnel. He waited until the boy was only a few feet away and then said, 'Welcome, welcome. I don't often get visitors. Sit down for a while, and tell me why you were inspecting my tunnel.'

'Is it your tunnel?' asked Ranji.

'It is,' said the watchman. 'It is truly my tunnel, since no one else will have anything to do with it. I have only lent it to the Government.'

Ranji sat down on the edge of the cot.

'I wanted to see the train come through,' he said. 'And then, when it had gone, I decided to walk through the tunnel.'

'And what did you find in it?'

'Nothing. It was very dark. But when I came out, I thought I saw an animal—up on the hill—but I'm not sure, it moved off very quickly.'

'It was a leopard you saw,' said the watchman. 'My leopard.'

'Do you own a leopard too?'

'I do.'

'And do you lend it to the Government?'

'I do not.'

'Is it dangerous?'

'Not if you leave it alone. It comes this way for a few days every month, because there are still deer in this jungle, and the deer is its natural prey. It keeps away from people.'

'Have you been here a long time?' asked Ranji.

'Many years. My name is Kishan Singh.'

'Mine is Ranji.'

'There is one train during the day. And there is one train during the night. Have you seen the Night Mail come through the tunnel?'

'No. At what time does it come?'

'About nine o'clock, if it isn't late. You could come and sit here with me, if you like. And after it has gone, I will take you home.'

'I'll ask my parents,' said Ranji. 'Will it be safe?'

'It is safer in the jungle than in the town. No rascals out here. Only last week, when I went into the town, I had my pocket picked! Leopards don't pick pockets.'

Kishan Singh stretched himself out on his cot. 'And now I am going to take a nap, my friend. It is too hot to be up and about in the afternoon.'

'Everyone goes to sleep in the afternoon,' complained Ranji. 'My father lies down as soon as he's had his lunch.'

'Well, the animals also rest in the heat of the day. It is only the tribe of boys who cannot, or will not, rest.'

Kishan Singh placed a large banana-leaf over his face to keep away the flies, and was soon snoring gently. Ranji stood up, looking up and down the

railway tracks. Then he began walking back to the village.

The following evening, towards dusk, as the flying-foxes swooped silently out of the trees, Ranji made his way to the watchman's hut.

It had been a long hot day, but now the earth was cooling and a light breeze was moving through the trees. It carried with it the scent of mango blossom, the promise of rain.

Kishan Singh was waiting for Ranji. He had watered his small garden and the flowers looked cool and fresh. A kettle was boiling on an oil-stove.

'I am making tea,' he said. 'There is nothing like a glass of hot sweet tea while waiting for a train.'

They drank their tea, listening to the sharp notes of the tailor-bird and the noisy chatter of the seven-sisters. As the brief twilight faded, most of the birds fell silent. Kishan lit his oil-lamp and said it was time for him to inspect the tunnel. He moved off towards the dark entrance, while Ranji sat on the cot, sipping tea.

In the dark, the trees seemed to move closer. And the night life of the forest was conveyed on the breeze—the sharp call of a barking-deer, the cry of a fox, the quaint tonk-tonk of a nightjar.

There were some sounds that Ranji would not recognize—sounds that came from the trees, creakings, and whisperings, as though the trees were coming alive, stretching their limbs in the dark, shifting a little, flexing their fingers.

Kishan Singh stood outside the tunnel, trimming his lamp. The night sounds were familiar to him and he did not give them much thought; but something else— a padded footfall, a rustle of dry leaves—made him

stand still for a few seconds, peering into the darkness.
Then, humming softly, he returned to where Ranji was
waiting. Then minutes remained for the Night Mail to
arrive.

As the watchman sat down on the cot beside Ranji, a
new sound reached both of them quite distinctly—a
rhythmic sawing sound, as of someone cutting through
the branch of a tree.

'What's that?' whispered Ranji.

'It's the leopard,' said Kishan Singh. 'I think it's in
the tunnel.'

'The train will soon be here.'

'Yes, my friend. And if we don't drive the leopard
out of the tunnel, it will be run over by the engine.'

'But won't it attack us if we try to drive it out?'
asked Ranji, beginning to share the watchman's concern.

'It knows me well. We have seen each other many
times. I don't think it will attack. Even so, I will take
my axe along. You had better stay here, Ranji.'

'No, I'll come too. It will be better than sitting here
alone in the dark.'

'All right, but stay close behind me. And remember,
there is nothing to fear.'

Raising his lamp, Kishan Singh walked into the
tunnel, shouting at the top of his voice to try and scare
away the animal. Ranji followed close behind. But he
found he was unable to do any shouting; his throat had
gone quite dry.

They had gone about twenty paces into the tunnel
when the light from the lamp fell upon the leopard. It
was crouching between the tracks, only fifteen feet away
from them. Baring its teeth and snarling, it went down
on its belly, tail twitching. Ranji felt sure it was going
to spring at them.

Kishan Singh and Ranji both shouted together.

Their voices rang through the tunnel. And the leopard, uncertain as to how many terrifying humans were there in front of him, turned swiftly and disappeared into the darkness.

To make sure it had gone, Ranji and the watchman walked the length of the tunnel. When they returned to the entrance, the rails were beginning to hum. They knew the train was coming.

Ranji put his hand to one of the rails and felt its tremor. He heard the distant rumble of the train. And then the engine came round the bend, hissing at them, scattering sparks into the darkness, defying the jungle as it roared through the steep sides of the cutting. It charged straight into the tunnel, thundering past Ranji like the beautiful dragon of his dreams.

And when it had gone, the silence returned and the forest seemed to breathe, to live again. Only the rails still trembled with the passing of the train.

They trembled again to the passing of the same train, almost a week later, when Ranji and his father were both travelling in it.

Ranji's father was scribbling in a notebook, doing his accounts. How boring of him, thought Ranji as he sat near an open window staring out at the darkness. His father was going to Delhi on a business trip and had decided to take the boy along.

'It's time you learnt something about the business,' he had said, to Ranji's dismay.

The Night Mail rushed through the forest with its hundreds of passengers. The carriage wheels beat out a steady rhythm on the rails. Tiny flickering lights came and went, as they passed small villages on the fringe of the jungle.

Ranji heard the rumble as the train passed over a small bridge. It was too dark to see the hut near the cutting, but he knew they must be approaching the tunnel. He strained his eyes, looking out into the night; and then, just as the engine let out a shrill whistle, Ranji saw the lamp.

He couldn't see Kishan Singh, but he saw the lamp, and he knew that his friend was out there.

The train went into the tunnel and out again, it left the jungle behind and thundered across the endless plains. And Ranji stared out at the darkness, thinking of the lonely cutting in the forest, and the watchman with the lamp who would always remain a fire-fly for those travelling thousands, as he lit up the darkness for steam-engines and leopards.

Train of Ghosts

DOUGLAS HILL

Davy waited for two cars to pass before riding across the highway. After pedalling slowly up a steep path, he coasted down the other side, past the edge of town.

Between the town and a sweep of woods lay a broad, open strip of land stretching as far as Davy could see in either direction. It was peaceful there, silent except for a breeze and the summer noises of birds and bugs. But it hadn't always been like that.

The empty strip of land was where the railroad used to run.

And what especially drew Davy there was the fact that it was said to be *haunted*. By ghostly leftovers from the days when steam engines hauled trains past Davy's town, east of Canada's Great Lakes.

The days of steam were long gone, as the railroad itself was gone from that strip of land. The old station, its wooden platform, the rails, all had been torn up long before. Yet people still sometimes heard spooky sounds—metal wheels clattering on rails, the *chuff-chuff*

of an engine leaning into its labours, the shivery cry of a whistle on a winter night . . .

Davy badly wanted to hear it, too, spooky or not. He loved everything to do with trains, especially old steam engines. He was willing to be a bit scared, if he could hear even the tiniest ghost of a sound from those days.

As he braked to a stop, he saw that for once he didn't have the place to himself. A man was sitting on a grassy hummock, by the woods.

As Davy peered, the man raised a friendly hand. 'Afternoon, young feller,' he said. 'You here to meet the train?'

It was an odd question, Davy thought. And the man—grey-haired with a large stomach—looked odd as well. He wore overalls, work shirt, and a high-crowned cap like the steam-engine drivers, the *engineers*, wore in the old days. But his cap and overalls weren't normal blue denim. They looked like *camouflage* gear, even his shirt—exactly like the leaves and grass around him.

Davy wasn't supposed to speak to strangers, odd or not. But he was an athletic eleven-year-old on a bike, knowing he could move faster than any fat old man. 'What train?' he demanded. 'There aren't even any *tracks.*'

The man seemed to smile, though it was hard to tell with his cap shadowing his face. 'There are for this train,' he said.

'You mean the *ghost* train?' Davy asked. 'Have you heard it?'

The old man chuckled, getting slowly to his feet. And Davy went stiff and still and icy cold.

It wasn't camouflage that made the man's clothes look like the leaves and grass. It was because Davy could *see through him*.

'Heard it?' the man smiled. 'Son, I've come to *catch* it.'

He took a drifting step forward—which snapped Davy out of his frozen stillness. Gasping, he swung his bike around and raced away, up the slope towards the town. And he was still pedalling hard, desperate to get away, as he fled down the steep path on the far side.

He didn't see the truck as he flashed out on to the highway. He didn't even feel anything, after the one shattering impact that flung him into silence, and darkness . . .

Until he found himself back on the bare strip of land at the edge of town. Where two others had joined the old engineer—a tiny white-haired woman in a stiff black dress, and a tall white-haired man in an old-fashioned suit. Both of them also hazily transparent.

'Sorry I made you run, son,' the old engineer murmured.

The old woman sniffed. 'Nothing to be *sorry* about. Likely it was just his time.'

Looking down, Davy saw that he too had become transparent. Yet he felt only a wisp of alarm, only a touch of sadness. His feelings seemed *muffled*, like voices through plate glass.

'Am I dead, then?' he asked.

The old engineer shook his head. 'What we say is, we've left the First-life, an' started our Next-life. In the natural way of things. You might feel sad for a while, missin' your folks an' all, but it won't last.' He smiled. 'We may not be too *solid*, but we're lively enough.'

'Some of us,' the old woman said, 'think we're better off, here. You'll see, boy, in time.' Something gleeful

flickered in her eyes. 'Specially if you come on the
train. There might be a *surprise* for you, at the end of
the line.'

The old engineer looked uneasy. 'Hold on, Maud.
Oughtn't he stay here, near home? He might not be all
the way *across*, yet . . .'

'Nonsense!' the old woman snapped. 'The train's
just what he needs, to settle him.' But the hint of glee
still moved in her eyes.

'And here it comes,' said the tall old man, with a
leering grin.

Davy wanted to ask about the mysterious surprise,
but was stopped—by the warning whistle of an
approaching train. At once, as if summoned by the
whistle, rails appeared on the strip of land, hazy
ribbons of steel on wooden ties half-buried in a ballast
of gravel. And they were standing on a misty wooden
platform, with a station behind it, looking as it must
have looked a hundred years before.

'D'you want to come, son?' the old engineer asked.

Davy hesitated. 'I guess so,' he said. 'I don't know
what else to do.'

The engineer nodded. 'You just stick by me, an'
you'll be fine.' He smiled. 'I'm called Casey, by the
way. From the song—'cause my last name's Jones an' I
was an engineer. An' this is Maud, an' Walter.'

'My name's Davy,' Davy said. 'About that surprise . . .'

But he stopped, filled with wondering delight as the
train arrived in a thunderous storm of sound. Davy had
seen old steam engines silent and idle in museums, but
this . . . Although it was also hazy and misty, it seemed
alive. An immense, glorious, powerful beast, snorting as
it stopped, brakes squealing, steam hissing like giant
gusts of breath as it muttered and clanked, seeming
eager to thunder away again.

And, Davy saw, it was a *passenger* train. With a hazy conductor bringing down the portable step that let people climb on to the high coach, while misty faces smiled from the windows.

'Not just a ghost train, but a trainful of ghosts,' Casey chuckled.

'Where's it going?' Davy asked.

'West, all the way,' Casey said. 'Coast to coast. An' that's a trip nobody in First-life can do any more.'

'Lots of things they can't do,' Maud muttered.

On the train, where the misty passengers made a bit of a fuss of Davy, they took their seats—Maud and Walter opposite Davy and Casey—as the engine huffed and whistled and slid smoothly away.

'In my day,' Casey told Davy, 'steam trains took a lot of days an' nights, goin' coast to coast. It's thousands of miles.' He winked. 'But this train's different.'

'Most everything's different in Next-life,' old Walter said, grinning.

'And better,' Maud sniffed.

'Maybe,' Casey said, frowning. 'Anyways, Davy, this train goes faster'n you'd believe, but you'll see everythin' as clear as if it was crawlin'. Don't ask me how.' He grinned. 'An' it's worth seein'. This country's a great big beautiful place.'

So Davy eagerly leaned to the window, all thought of Maud's surprise driven from his mind.

The journey began on the fierce stony land above and beyond the Lakes, a thousand miles of forested wilderness where the train seemed to be rushing endlessly along a narrow green tunnel. But sometimes the forest opened out, briefly, to show a sunlit lake, a paved highway, a small lonely town.

Davy saw that the ghost train was running past, or

through, the real places and things of what Casey called First-life. But also, he often saw ghostly shapes out of the past—crude pioneer shacks, dusty streets with shadowy horses and wagons . . .

'Do we stop anywhere?' Davy asked.

'Maybe, to pick up more passengers,' Casey said. 'But not for coal or water. This engine doesn't ever run out. Doesn't break down, either.'

'Just like us,' Walter chortled. 'We don't get hungry now, nor sleepy.'

'And that's another blessing,' Maud said firmly.

By then Davy had realized what Casey had meant about things being different. He had time to look at things as closely as he wanted—yet the train was moving at incredible speed. It should have taken a day and a night and another half-day, Casey said, to get past the lakehead. But it was only about two *hours* before the wilderness began to thin out, beyond the Lakes.

And only minutes later, they burst out on to the vastness of the western plains.

'That's better,' Walter grunted. 'I hate all that forest.'

'Some of us like it well enough,' Casey said, frowning. 'But the prairies are good too. You ever see so much *sky*, Davy?'

'It's too flat,' Maud sniffed. 'Flat and boring.'

But Davy wasn't bored, as the train swept along. He was enchanted—watching cloud-shadows sweeping across the land, the rippling patterns made by the wind on the immense wheatfields, a meadowlark singing on a fencepost, furry gophers tumbling around their burrows . . .

And amid all that, among the modern towns and cities with strange names, Davy saw more ghostly glimpses of the past—a settler's hut made of sods cut from the land, a clutch of tepees by a stream, a gigantic herd of buffalo stretching to the far horizon.

But in another two hours or so, the land grew steeply rolling, until in the distance Davy saw where the prairies ended. A jagged, white-capped wall of mountains, like a row of sharpened teeth.

'There's the Rockies,' Walter grinned.

'And past the mountains we're at the coast,' Maud said. '*That's* the part I like about these trips.' She glanced at Davy with a small gleeful smile. 'And that's where you'll get your surprise, young man.'

'Won't you tell me what it is?' Davy begged.

Walter snickered. 'Wouldn't be a surprise, then, would it?'

'But is it some kind of *present* or something?' Davy asked.

'No,' Maud sniffed. 'It's just . . . well, you'll see.'

Casey frowned suspiciously. 'What're you an' Walter up to, Maud?'

'Nothing at all,' Maud snapped. 'And it's no concern of yours. The boy will find out, soon enough.'

By then the train's astounding speed brought it into the shaggy foothills, then up among the crags of the Rocky Mountains. Davy stared with awe at the towering peaks, the dizzy cliffs and ledges, the ridges covered with frosty glaciers like icing on a cake . . . And at the lower slopes, all wild forests and foaming rivers, where beavers built sturdy dams and bears clawed fish from the water.

Before long they were racing down again, towards a coastal city, a bright jewel in the setting of the mountains with the blue Pacific beyond. The train flashed through the city's gleaming streets, where Davy glimpsed ghostly log cabins and whiskery frontiersmen among the skyscrapers and shiny cars. Until, finally, they rolled into a hazy smoke-darkened station, and stopped.

'End of the line,' Casey said. 'What'd you think of that, Davy?'

'Oh . . . ' Davy could hardly find words. 'It's the most wonderful train ride *ever*.'

'That it is,' Casey agreed. 'An' it's a cryin' shame that no one in First-life can ever take that coast-to-coast ride again.'

Maud sniffed. 'That's the trouble with First-life. Folks keep ruining things.'

Casey nodded sadly. 'Things changed, sure enough. People take planes, now, 'cause they're faster, or buses 'cause they're cheaper, or they drive cars. An' they send freight on trucks. So the old main lines weren't makin' money . . . An' now there's not much left but local lines, an' a few bits here an' there for tourists.' He smiled. 'But it's all still here for us, just like it was.'

'Better,' Maud snapped.

Davy sighed. 'So what do we do now?'

'We can drift around here a while, if you like,' Casey said. 'Later on we'll take the return trip. You can look out of the window on the other side!'

'And,' Maud said with a pinched smile, 'you can enjoy your surprise.'

'Great,' Davy said. 'What is it?'

Maud looked gleeful. 'I thought Casey might notice before now.'

'What're you talkin' about?' Casey demanded.

She sniffed. 'You're a fool, Casey. You've been in Next-life nearly as long as Walter and me, and you still don't know the signs when you see them.'

'Signs?' Casey repeated. Then he looked at Davy,

and his face crumpled with horror. 'Oh, Davy! I'm sorry! I didn't *see* . . . !'

Again Davy looked down at himself, and shock struck him like a club. On all the edges of his transparent body he saw tiny points of light, glowing softly.

'What is it?' he gasped.

'It means,' Casey whispered, 'you're not all the way into Next-life yet. It means you're tryin' to get *back*. To your . . . your body.'

'But you won't make it,' Walter grinned. 'You're too far away.'

Maud cackled. 'In about half an hour, it'll be too late. You'll be here to stay.'

'And you two *knew*, all along,' Casey said angrily, 'an' didn't *say*!'

'Why should we?' Maud sniffed. 'Who'd go back to First-life when they could be here? He should thank us!'

'Nobody *made* him catch the train,' Walter sneered.

Casey loomed to his feet, glaring. 'You two . . . !' he growled. 'You've been gettin' meaner an' nastier year by year, turnin' everythin' sour . . . And now you've done this cruel thing. Maud, I think you an' Walter better go. Take your meanness somewhere else. Stay away from this train, an' stay away from Davy an' me.'

'Yes, go on, get out!' cried a chorus of voices, and Davy saw that all the others had clustered around, glaring.

'Fine,' Maud snorted. 'Who wants to stay around a lot of fools who're too stupid to see we've done the boy a *favour*?'

And with a sniff and a leer she and Walter drifted out of the coach, and away.

Davy's misty body was trembling, his hazy eyes filling with tears. 'But I really *want* to go back . . . '

'I know, Davy,' Casey groaned. 'But it's *hours* back to your home town . . . ' He paused, frowning. 'Wait, though. I've known that engine go faster'n we went today. An' I've never found out what its *top* speed is.'

Davy stared with desperate hope.

'An' who better,' Casey cried, 'to take it to top speed than an engineer named Casey Jones?' His laugh was a roar. 'Come on, Davy, let's see how far we can get in the time that's left!'

Grabbing Davy's hand, he plunged towards the front of the train. Somehow the ghostly engine had got turned around, facing back the way it had come, ready to go as Casey pulled Davy up into the grimy cab.

'Hang on!' he roared, as he reached for the long shiny lever that was the throttle, and pulled.

The engine leaped forward like a charging beast. Steadily Casey pulled the throttle back and back, as far as it would go. Then with all his ghostly strength he battled to open it another impossible inch, and another . . .

Misty wheels barely touching hazy rails, the engine shrieked across the land like a colossal blazing missile. Clinging to the fireman's seat, Davy saw only a blur as they hurtled into the mountains—and out again in moments, storming down to the plains. Faster and faster the engine went, its boiler groaning as if about to explode, until in no time they were plunging through the eastern forest. Astonished and fearful, Davy cried out to Casey, but his voice was drowned by a monstrous, agonized screech.

Casey was slamming on the brakes—and in another instant they had come to a stop. On the grassy strip of land by the woods, at the edge of Davy's town.

'Well, now,' Casey said softly. 'Who would've guessed the train could move like *that*? Not old Maud, for sure.' He chuckled. 'An' we didn't wreck it, either, like Casey Jones in the song.'

Davy looked down. The points of light around his edges were much brighter, and were spreading. 'What do I do?' he whispered.

'It'll happen by itself,' Casey said gently.

'Will I . . . ever see you again?' Davy asked.

'Sure,' Casey said, 'but not for a long while. I reckon you'll be older'n me when you finally come over to stay.' He grinned. 'An' the train an' me will still be here.'

Suddenly Davy seemed to be floating, blinking in the light pouring from his misty form. Then he squeezed his eyes shut as the light flared even more dazzlingly, with a deep musical throb like the boom of a massive drum.

When he opened his eyes again, he found himself in a hospital bed, bandages around his head and ribs, plaster casts gripping one leg up to the knee and one arm up to the shoulder. And by the bed stood his mother and father.

'He's *awake*!' they gasped, together, wide-eyed with startled joy.

'Well, well,' a white-coated doctor said, leaning past them to peer at Davy. 'You had us worried, young man. We weren't sure we'd get you back.'

'I had a train ride,' Davy whispered. 'All across the country, to the coast.'

'That sounds like a good dream,' his father said shakily.

I guess it does, Davy thought, smiling to himself. Trains can't make that trip, here in the real world. But it *wasn't* a dream. There *is* a train, for the ghosts. And I *will* ride it again, one day.

But, as Casey said, not for a long while . . .

Corder's Spur

MARJORIE DARKE

'What's got into you this morn, Jem, you be slow as a snail!'

Jem pulled on his hobnailed boots and laced them up.

'Be you listening to me? None of your gawping through the window at that railway . . . and don'ee forget your grub neither!' About to leave for washday at the Big House, his mam paused: 'DID'EE HEAR ME?'

They could hear her down Copperstone most like, Jem thought. Grabbing the knotted rag that held his slab of bread and lard from the kitchen table, he waved it at her.

The door banged.

Buttoning his jacket, Jem tucked the grub inside, then pulled on his cap. It was his dad's old cap, a dirty grey from years of wear working at Corder's sawmill, and came down over Jem's ears, but he didn't care. It kept out the weather. He paused a moment for a quick forbidden glance through the window. Ever since the

navvies came all of four years ago, carrying their
picks and shovels to start digging their way through
the fields, he had been captivated. Every chance that
came his way he'd steal closer and watch the heavy
horses carting loads of earth, and hauling the
gleaming rails.

'Like a wasp after plums,' his mam grumbled time
and again.

The railway was finished now, the navvies long gone
after laying the last sleeper . . .

' . . . on Queen Victoria's birthday, poor soul!' Mam
had made it sound like an insult.

Though it was early October, usually there was a
clear view of the track running across the embankment
where the land dipped down into the river valley.
Today rain slashed the windowpanes and a curtain of
mist cut off any sight of the railway.

The door creaked open again. Mam poked her head
in long enough to say: 'And don'ee lollop about
daydreaming or you'll be late. Your dad and our Billy
be long gone.'

Jem started guiltily. Had she seen where he'd been
looking? She hated the railway and the fiery smoking
engines. 'Devil machines' she called them. Most of the
villagers felt the same way. So did Squire up at the Big
House, but for a different reason. He wasn't scared,
just angry at his land being taken.

Jem lifted the sack kept for wet days from the nail
behind the door. It was split open one side and he
draped it over his cap and shoulders.

Outside the rain hit him smartly in the face. Hard,
driving rain that filled the potholes and made little
rivers as he splashed along the village street. Here and
there a candle still glowed through a window. He
envied the people indoors, dry and warm, supping their

tea, eating bread and bacon dip while he tramped towards the day's work of picking stones.

Head bent, he began to hurry towards Beechdyke Farm. There wasn't a hope of work in the dry barns, but he knew he must show his face to Gaffer before carrying on to Hod's Piece field.

They met as Jem tramped across the farmyard.

'What time do you call this, boy?' Farmer Bowditch brought out his round turnip pocket watch and tapped the glass.

Not having any sort of clock at home, Jem was tempted to say 'Morning,' but didn't want to risk a clip round the ear.

'Twenty to seven!' Gaffer said for him. 'By now you should've worked near three quarters of an hour, m'lad! Well, you've been late once too often. Here's your wage. Not that you deserve a full week, seeing it's only Thursday, so think yourself lucky!' he felt in his pocket. 'Now be off with you.'

'But, sir . . . them stones . . . ' In a daze, Jem took the shilling held out.

Farmer Bowditch gave a snorting laugh. 'Don't you worry about that. I've a new lad. Living in. He won't oversleep if he knows what's good for him.'

A new lad? Jem's mind raced through the village, but he couldn't think of any lad over six years not already in work.

And then he saw the back door of the farm open letting out a thin scarecrow figure. A tattered jacket came well down over the knees of his ragged trousers. His feet were lost in outsize boots. No cap on his head, and the rain was changing his mop of carroty curls to a darker red. As the boy wiped his hand across his mouth a memory stirred, disappearing before Jem could fish it out.

Hearing the latch click, Farmer Bowditch turned.
'Tolly! Come over. This here's Jem. He'll take you
up Hod's Piece,' and to Jem: 'Show him what to do
. . . but don't hang about once the lad knows what
he's at. I'll be up afore long, so no larking or I'll
have both your hides!' and taking them by the
shoulders, Gaffer gave them a shove towards the farm
gate.

Tramping along the lane, neither said a word. Jem
was trying to think what he would tell them at home.
But could think of no way round the truth. He'd lost
his job! He'd got his week's shilling but that was the
end.

He shivered.

The rain had begun to ease and Jem pushed back
his hood for a better look at the scarecrow who had
filched his job. 'You ain't from round here,' he said
accusingly.

Tolly gave him a shifty look.

'Lost your tongue?' Jem asked truculently.

The boy hung his head, trudging on, shoulders
hunched.

'You'll not last more'n a couple of days. Three at
the outside,' Jem taunted. 'You ain't got no muscles.'
He knew he was being mean, but fury and fright made
him want to give the scrawny pipsqueak a punch in the
mouth.

'Is Hod's Piece what they are calling the meadow at
the back of the railway?' Tolly asked suddenly.

The husky voice with its Irish lilt did the trick. A
picture of Hod's Piece when it was a green field covered
with the navvie camp swam into Jem's head. Men
digging out earth for the embankment, their arms like
tree trunks. Women cooking over camp fires. Snot-nosed
kids yelling and charging about—Tolly one of them.

He was taller now, stringier, but otherwise much the same.

'I remember you! You're the kid who chucked a stone at me,' Jem frowned. 'Where's your mam and dad?'

Tolly looked away, mouth turned down. 'What's it got to do with you where they are,' he muttered.

Jem remembered how the camp children had seemed like one great screaming family. 'You've run off, haven't you!' the quick frightened glance told him he'd landed on the truth.

'You won't be telling Gaffer,' Tolly said with a touch of belligerence.

'Why? Scared he'll send you packing?'

'I can't be going back . . . I will not go back, not if Satan himself gave the order! Do what you like, you can't make me.' With rain running down his cheeks and dripping off his sharp nose, Tolly looked so like a little animal backed into a corner Jem felt a twinge of pity. Then his heart hardened. But for this pipsqueak, Gaffer might have shouted and given him a cuff, but nothing more.

Tolly's small green eyes were darting from side to side. Jem could almost smell fear. 'What you been up to? Thieving bread . . . scrumping apples? Gaffer won't stand for kids as bring trouble.'

'Sure I never said a word about being in trouble. If anyone is in trouble it will be you with no work to do,' Tolly seemed to get his second wind. 'And don't you put the fault on my back. 'Twas not me as made you late this morn.'

Surprised by the unexpected attack, Jem couldn't find a ready answer. He walked on sullenly. The thought of telling at home how he'd lost his job was enough to make *him* run off! He could almost feel the cut of Dad's belt across his legs.

They had come to the footbridge over the river. Crossing it they went up the wandering lane towards the embankment. The mist was thinner now, and the rain had shrunk to a drizzle that pitted the surface of the brimming ditches. Sheep bleated in the field beyond a hedge, small black faces peering through a gate.

The railway station was not far off. Jem's gloom began to lift. He could just see the roof of the single storey stone building where passengers sheltered and Bert Davis sold tickets and boiled his tea-kettle on a little iron stove. Beyond lay Hod's Piece, then thick green woods stretching up to the horizon, concealing Corder's sawmill. Jem knew it all as well as he knew his own feet and hands. Any moment they would see Corder's Spur, a single line track, branching from the main line round the edge of Hod's Piece into the woods.

Often Jem watched wagons piled with planks being pulled by a little tank engine along the spur to join the main line at the junction. From there the train chuntered on to Copperstone—sometimes travelling as far as Glastonbury. He liked to imagine them going even further until they reached the Great Western Railway! Given half a chance, Bert would talk endlessly about the mighty 'GWR', though where it began and where it ended remained a mystery.

Suddenly Jem raised his head to sniff the air.

Tolly noticed. 'What can you smell? Is it a fox?'

Jem gave him a scornful look. ''Tis engine smoke!'

'Well sure, that's what you'd expect when we are coming to the railway!'

'There's no train this early.'

'How can you be knowing that?'

'I know all the train times on this line.'

'And aren't you the clever one!'

'Oh, shut your mouth and listen!' Jem's nose didn't often let him down. Nor his ears. He sniffed again. Strained after sounds. Yes—a train all right!

'I'll be having to sit down for a minute,' Tolly complained.

'What?' For an instant Jem had forgotten Tolly existed. He saw the pipsqueak was limping. 'Now what's wrong?'

'A sharp stone walked into me boot,' Tolly lifted his outsize boot, showing that the sole had partly come away from the upper.

'Sit down and take it off!' A simple enough request that seemed to take forever. 'Give it I!'

When the stone was out and the boot back on, Jem rapidly tied the sole to the upper with a length of string from his pocket. But that was all he was prepared to do. Anxious not to miss seeing the unexpected train, he left Tolly to look after himself.

At last the station came into sight above a scrub of dripping bushes. The rain had finally stopped allowing Jem to see across the line to Corder's Spur and beyond. He was just about to turn and look for the oncoming train, when he glimpsed something that made his blood freeze.

Flapping up behind, Tolly saw it too. 'LOOK!' he bellowed. 'Over there . . . beyond the junction . . . 'tis a landslip or I'm blind as a mole. And there's a train coming up the track as if the Devil was after it . . . with the signal saying come on.'

The red eye of the signal disc with its crossbar beneath stood sideways-on to the track. As good as a beckoning finger to any train driver. Puzzled, Jem scanned the station looking for Bert's bulky figure. Not a sign, nor a wisp of smoke from the chimney to say he was boiling his kettle.

Time was shrinking.

'Find the stationmaster. Tell him I've gone to switch the signal.' Throwing off the sack, Jem began to run.

Tolly clopped after him. 'Where will he be?'

'How should I know! Use your eyes.'

With his longer legs, Jem was first on to the platform. Still not a sign of Bert.

The signal was a stone's throw beyond the end of the platform. Time and again Jem had watched Bert use the bar at its base to swivel the disc. It was easy enough.

The sound of the engine was growing more distinct.

Reaching the signal Jem grasped the bar, only to have his wet hands slip with the first pull. He rubbed them on his chest and tried again using all his strength, but the pole refused to budge. Only then did he realize that it was not resting true in the socket and had jammed. He wondered if somebody had set out to wreck it? He began to sweat. Trying to right the pole might be a long job. The red eye of the disc seemed to jeer down at him.

'Bloody thing!' he muttered, as a first little plume of steam and smoke rose above the slope. His heart began to thump. Even if the signal said 'STOP' the train would have trouble halting before reaching the landslip.

Pounding back up the platform he could see how it would be—engine ploughing into the mud; wheels slipping off the track; wagons overturning; driver and fireman thrown out . . . maybe killed . . .

'Tolly!' he yelled, slowing a fraction to be sure of being heard. 'Tell Bert the signal's out of action.'

Tolly's anxious face poked round the side of the station hut. ''Tis no good. He's been having a fall . . . I found him back here . . . says he's hurt his leg . . . I don't know if he can walk . . . '

Jem stopped listening. Glancing back along the track he saw the drifting plumes fatten against the sky. Any minute the train would be clacking through the station! What was he going to do? Shouting was useless! By the time the engine reached the platform it would be too late. Even if the driver saw the mountain of mud for himself he wouldn't be able to stop in time!

Tolly ran after him, shouting something that sounded like 'beaver' . . .

The word beat in Jem's head in time with his footsteps. Beaver beaver beaver *lever* . . .

No breath to tell Tolly he understood. A giant hand seemed to squeeze his lungs making the last fifty yards seem like fifty miles. The increasing noise of the engine drummed in his ears. In his mind was an image of Bert, forearms swelling with effort as he switched the points so the wagons from the sawmill could run on to the main line . . .

One last glance . . .

The engine breasted the top of the slope as Jem arrived at the junction. A final rub at sweaty hands, heels digging into the gravel, he gripped the shoulder-high lever and *heaved*. The rails shifted . . . but not enough. Despair swept through him. The tracks were separated . . . the train would be derailed . . . one disaster swapped for another . . .

Eyes screwed tight, he gave one final HEAVE!

With extraordinary suddenness the lever slammed into place. Tumbling backwards, Jem opened his eyes, saw Tolly sprawled on the throbbing ground, heard the powerful clank of metal, caught a whiff of red hot coals mingled with a rich odour of oil, and felt the warm wind of the engine's passage as it ran smoothly on to Corder's Spur.

They looked at each other, breathing hard.

Jem gulped. 'That were a close shave! I'd not have done it without your shove.'

A slow grin spread across Tolly's face. 'I feared the engine will topple making a squash of us!'

They looked along Corder's Spur at the Vulcan grinding to a halt, bathed in steam. Jem saw an open tender piled with coal and the cap and shoulders of a fireman. Through the mist, the massive black body of the engine with brass-banded funnel and polished dome shone in the pale sunlight. Never had he seen anything so handsome, so *huge*! But it was the sheer power of the great wheels and gleaming steel connecting-rods that took his breath. A single carriage, two empty wagons, and the guard's van were coupled behind. Slowly the driver, then the guard, climbed down on to the track and began hurrying towards the junction, leaving the fireman craning from the footplate.

As Jem scrambled to his feet, Tolly grabbed his arm.

'Would you look who's coming up the lane! 'Tis Gaffer himself—and we're supposed to be in the field picking stones!'

Jem didn't need telling twice. Hissing: 'Keep to the track!' he headed for the station, meaning to nip out and across the lane to a familiar gap in the hedge that led into Hod's Piece.

'Hold hard!'

Gaffer's voice. Gaffer's bulk looming in front. Gaffer's vice of a hand gripping his shoulder.

'You an' all!'

Jem saw Gaffer's other hand grasp Tolly's jacket. Both were pinned like a couple of rabbits in a trap! He braced himself for the roar of anger—and remembered . . .

This man wasn't his Gaffer any longer!

Feeling for the shilling in his pocket, he turned it
for luck. ''Tisn't like you think. Tolly weren't hopping
off!'

The hand gripping his shoulder shook him. 'I know
that,' Farmer Bowditch growled. 'Though if I hadn't
seen with my own eyes I'd have thought different.'

The driver and guard arrived on the platform—then
Bert, using his stool to lean on and limp. They all
began talking at once.

'That were well done, lads . . . '

'A sharp pair of tacks as ever I saw . . . '

'How old are ye, lad?'

It took a second and another shake for Jem to realize
the driver meant *him*!

'Ten,' he croaked. 'Eleven at Christmas.'

'You come on down to Copperstone in the New
Year. Ask for Driver Hadfield. We could use a lad as
can think on his feet. D'you want to work on the
railway?'

Jem's legs felt suddenly weak. 'Oh, yes sir!' it was
the dream of his life!

'Don't forget then—bring your mate an' all.' The
driver turned away, talk swinging back to the landslip
and what was to be done.

Now nobody was bothering with them, Jem moved
away, suddenly tired. His stomach groaned with
hunger. Remembering the grub he fished it out,
untying the rag. Tolly's tongue licked round his lips.
Jem held out a hunk of bread.

'Want some?'

Tolly nodded.

Squatting together on the edge of the platform Jem
nudged him and winked. They grinned at each other.
Then set about gobbling the bread until the last crumb
was gone.

North

LAURENCE STAIG

The railway station was huge and it echoed with the soft voices of a thousand lost souls. Footsteps tapped on smooth tile, almost sounding like the 'clickety-clack' of a cruising train. The hurly-burly muffled hum of busy people sounded distant and unreal. Timmy peered up and up, into the ceiling of glass and steel. Birds were trapped in the roof, the flapping of their wings sounded urgent and desperate.

The vastness of the place reminded Timmy of a cathedral in Italy he had once visited with his parents; it had been in a little town just outside Rome. He remembered that the cathedral had been quieter, and there had been incense and shadows with pockets of darkness amongst a sea of tiny candles. The railway station was much brighter, lightning bright, yet to Timmy it was just the same as the cathedral: there was something about it.

People were milling everywhere, passing by with their eyes straight ahead. Everyone was on the move, except a person who stood nearby.

An elderly man dressed in a long black coat stood quietly. He wore a velvet black top hat which struggled to contain a generous amount of milky coloured hair. His face was turned away. For some reason he did not understand, Timmy suddenly wanted to see him properly. He was strangely dressed as though in some kind of costume. Timmy bit his lip and waited. After a moment he began to look round, as though aware he was being stared at, and as he turned a shudder ran through Timmy. Timmy looked away with a start. He didn't want to see him after all.

'Why, you poor darling,' said Auntie, her brow furrowing with concern. 'Whatever is the matter? And we thought you had got over that nasty bug too. Maybe you're not well enough for the journey after all. Or, perhaps it's the heat, yes—that's it; the weather is gorgeous after all. Why, your forehead's dripping wet.'

Timmy thought of the old man and his big black coat and nervously took a sidelong glance back to where he had been standing. But he had moved away.

Timmy looked up at his auntie. The sunlight, which streamed through the ceiling panes, backlit her and made her appear huge, like a great looming bird. She looked down at him, her face a blur within the oval of her hat. He had not noticed that he had been perspiring and rubbed the back of his hand across his forehead. For a second he felt dizzy.

'Just you wait there, a cool drink is what you need; but we must get a move on, your train is due in any moment.'

Auntie turned on her heels and made for a nearby refreshment stand, a trolley with candy coloured stripes and a marquee-style roof.

Timmy remained rooted to the spot. It was indeed an exceptionally hot day, in fact he could not remember

when he had felt this hot. He watched as Auntie bought a can of something from the man behind the stand who wore a straw boater and a pink striped apron. Within moments she had returned and handed him the dripping aluminium can.

'It's cold lemonade, darling. Just hold it against your head for a moment and I'm sure you will feel much cooler. Now let me see, where did I put your ticket?'

Timmy did as he was asked as Auntie stepped back and narrowed her eyes at the huge Departure Board, which hung above the station concourse. The metal can felt cold against his forehead and stung like an arrow of ice as he pressed it against his skin. He swallowed a dry dusty swallow and then drank as though he had spent hours in the desert. The rustle of the changing destination signs made him look up. The noise they made reminded him of the birds in the roof.

'Ah there you are, darling, platform seven and it seems that the train's in. Let's get you on board and settled.'

Timmy searched along the list of platform numbers and places. Trains appeared to be going everywhere, to all kinds of places all over the country, but nowhere could he see his destination. He blinked hard and the board seemed to waver like a ripple in a pond—then the fluttering place names rustled again.

'Come on, let's go,' shrilled Auntie as she picked up his small leather suitcase. 'Then I must be off.'

As if from nowhere hordes of people streamed out on to the concourse and, like a herd with a single mind, moved in the direction which Timmy and his auntie were taking. They were an unusual collection, different to the other passengers who had been passing by. A number of people were elderly, some taking small steps.

A few children moved slowly, though they seemed to
be coughing and having some difficulty. Others were
moving in an odd kind of way. He ran to catch up and
held on to the sleeve of Auntie's jacket.

'You'll be just fine, darling,' she said, as they briskly
weaved through the crowd. 'Don't you worry now. It's
a long journey, but just think of it, when you get there
tonight Mummy and Daddy will be waiting for you—
ready to take you to the new home they've been getting
ready.'

Timmy looked up and smiled. He hadn't seen his
parents for six months. This had been the longest time
ever without them. Although the school they had put
him in hadn't been that bad, he still missed them. They
had been abroad. 'Too dangerous for you to come with
us this time,' Daddy had said. The last posting had
been to a secret and risky part of the world. That was
sometimes the problem with Daddy's job. Timmy had
come back from school with this horrible bug too—but
he was getting better now. '*The good news is that it's the
last time*,' Daddy had said. '*We're buying a house in the
north and when it's ready we'll all meet up there. No
more travelling.*'

'No more travelling,' said Timmy to himself. How
he looked forward to that, no more strange countries
and no more strange schools too, where he had to try
and make friends all over again.

'Did you say something, darling?' said Auntie with a
smile.

Timmy shook his head.

Ahead of them the gates opened onto the platform.
They were made of thick black bars and the railings
appeared taller than usual, almost as though they were
the entrance to a country estate. One of the station
officials stood by the gates. He was busy checking

tickets but Timmy could see that he had a whistle in his mouth. Timmy looked up at him as they passed by, finding it difficult to look away.

'Hurry along, sonny,' he said without looking up. 'Time to go.'

'I just have to get him settled,' said Auntie, as she tugged at Timmy's hand and pulled him after her. He looked over his shoulder but the man was still busy with his face in the tickets.

They hurried along the platform past the silver blue coaches. Timmy felt hot again, his head thumped, and his mouth felt dry and sore as people ambled along beside them. Everyone in the world was boarding this train.

'There's a spot—just there!' said Auntie, pointing at an empty seat in the carriage.

She hurried him on to the train and put the little leather suitcase in a compartment behind his seat.

'And a lovely window seat too!' she said with a huge smile.

Just as he settled himself into the corner of the seat a lady with a soft black hat moved silently into the seat across from his. She had a veil which hung down in front of her eyes and was dressed as though she were going to some special occasion.

Timmy looked at her. Her lips were a bright ruby red.

'Don't stare, it's rude,' hissed Auntie. 'Now take care. Remember to take your capsules—finish the course as the doctor told you to and be sure to tell Mummy if you aren't feeling better. Auntie must be off, now that you're settled.'

Timmy looked around him, all of the seats were taken now. People were huddled into their coats, despite the heat of the morning. Nobody appeared to

be looking at anyone else, it was as though each person were in their own little world.

'Everyone is so odd,' he said.

'Shush now,' said Auntie with some embarrassment.

A little girl who was breathing rather loudly moved into a seat across the aisle. She didn't look at Timmy.

'There you go,' Auntie remarked with a gesture towards the girl. 'A friend perhaps? Have you got your comic, now?'

Timmy nodded and felt in his jacket pocket for the rolled up comic. He turned towards the platform. The station official who had been at the gate now stood beside the carriage window. His back was turned away from the carriage, watching for a signal to blow his whistle.

Timmy never looked at Auntie as she kissed him on his forehead and hurried away. For a moment she stood beside the station official. Timmy stared at the man's back. His hair was bundled up into his hat and it bothered Timmy for some reason. He heard the doors roll shut with a comfortable thud.

He turned to face the woman who sat opposite and tried to smile. Her veil was like a dark curtain, the ruby lips were perfect—but they were still and did not smile in return.

The blast of the whistle made him jump and his little heart suddenly sounded huge in his ears. He reached for a tissue which was stuffed into the same pocket as his comic and he wiped his burning forehead. The train moved smoothly out of the station. It glided on its journey like a ship leaving the harbour.

Timmy looked back along the platform to see his auntie. But she had left and only the station official remained. He tried to see past him, back to the gates, but there was nobody else and no sign of Auntie. The

station had suddenly become deserted. He sat back in his seat and tried to swallow again. The horrible dryness in his throat had returned. For a moment he closed his eyes.

The train sped through the countryside. He had travelled on trains many times before but this train journey felt different. It was only after an hour or so that he realized that nobody had spoken. Everyone had sat quietly and stiffly as though they were patients in a waiting room. He thought back to his recent stay at the hospital and how he had waited for ages to be seen by the doctor. Everyone had sat silently staring at their feet and at the walls. It was just like that.

He opened up his comic and started to read. Occasionally he would look up at the lady opposite. He tried hard to see beyond her veil, trying to make out her eyes—but he could see nothing. It was going to be a long journey.

After another hour the train slowed. Timmy had gone into a daydream. He was feeling increasingly hot and had been unable to settle down to read his comic. All of a sudden he realized that the train was pulling in to a station. He gazed through the window. The weather had changed from a summer's day to a strange kind of autumn. The sky was a sickly yellow. He tried to catch the station name but had missed it. The lady opposite quietly picked up her bag and shifted out from her seat. A number of other people also made to move and followed her out to the doors. Half of the train appeared to be alighting here. The woman with the veil passed by his window. For a moment she turned towards Timmy. He caught his breath, thinking he had glimpsed her face behind the veil, but there had been

nothing there, just smooth pinkness as though her features had been removed.

The doors shut and the train moved on.

He looked about him. There were fewer people left in the carriage although the little girl still sat in her seat. She might be travelling on her own, like him.

'Hallo,' he said, peering his head round the seat. But she ignored him.

'Are you going north?' he asked realizing what a silly question he had asked: where else could the train be going?

She said nothing. It had been as though he wasn't there and he felt shy and embarrassed.

He stared out of the window again. The train had moved out into the countryside. There were flat empty acres of space, and there was no sign of villages or people. He wondered in what part of the country they might be. After a moment a puzzling thought occurred to him. Many people had got off the train, but nobody had got on. He shrugged his shoulders dismissively and looked at his watch; it must be time to take his medicine. The hands showed 12.00. Timmy frowned, that had been when they had boarded the train. His watch must have broken. Feeling very fed up and suddenly unwell again, he decided to try and sleep.

When Timmy awoke the sky outside had become overcast like a blanket of dark grey. He also felt distinctly cold and his hands and feet felt numb. There were fewer people than ever on the train now, so he thought he must have slept through one of the stops. He stood up and looked about him. It had also become significantly darker as though a thunderstorm might be brewing. His sense of time and space felt horribly misshapen. Doubts about the journey began to nag away at him. He did not feel right at all.

The train slowed for a moment. He looked across the aisle for the little girl—perhaps she would know where they were. Without his watch he felt lost. She must have moved for she was no longer sitting there. He searched the seats ahead, but still there was no sign of her. Timmy frowned and sat back in his seat; outside the encroaching night-time was racing the train.

'We must be there soon,' he said, his voice almost cracking.

He felt tears well up and he felt cold—the air around him trembled. He shut his eyes and hoped that when he opened them they would be up north. Please.

The train sped faster and faster through the deep dark night. Timmy was shivering quite badly now and had turned up the collar of his jacket. The lights were dimmer than earlier and they buzzed and faded as though the supply were about to give out.

He stared through the window. His own face reflected back—a grey paste mask with dark holes for eyes. For just a second he wondered whether it really was his own reflection and with a startled turn of his head he looked behind him. But there was nobody else there. The carriage was completely empty. He stood up and looked down the aisle to the end window. There was nobody in the connecting carriage either. He ran to the end and pushed the button for the door to open. Nothing happened.

He returned to his seat and looked out of the window again, eyes searching for signs of a town. There were only a few stars now, just visible above the distant mountains. The moon was a huge blood orange disc which hung low in the night sky, just visible between the twin peaks. Timmy moved back from the window and lifted his hand to the glass. It was cold, a pattern of ice crystals were beginning to spread from the place that he had touched.

'But it's the summer,' he murmured as he stared at the glass. 'How?'

He felt another shiver ripple through his body and then finally the lights flickered and went out.

The carriage was like a tomb.

He cried out, he was unable to help himself. But with the darkness of the carriage he was at least able to see outside more clearly. The train was about to enter a valley. The encroaching sides of the mountains were steeper than ever here. He pressed his face against the window. Despite the coldness he desperately wanted to see something out there that looked like a sign of life, the comfort of street lights, cars maybe. Something. Anything.

The slow sense of panic which had been building within him like a creeping fear now made him feel empty and deeply afraid. The mountains screened the night sky like a canopy and the cold inside the carriage was much, much worse.

'Soon be there, soon be there,' he murmured, trying desperately to give himself some grain of comfort, no matter how small. He looked at his watch again, and with a heavy feeling remembered that it had broken.

All of a sudden the carriage jolted, as if brakes had been applied, and the train began to slow down. Timmy's heart beat faster. Perhaps they were pulling into the station at last. He looked out of the window again searching for signs of an approaching platform. It was darker than ever and even the passing countryside was invisible as though a cloak had dropped from the sky.

There was another jolt and the carriage lights flickered into life again as the train eased into a slower speed. Timmy gasped and, without reaching for his suitcase, he scrambled out of his seat into the aisle and along to the carriage doors.

The train was definitely stopping. They were finally pulling into a station. He coughed and spluttered, his mouth felt drier than ever, his head thumped harder. How he longed to get off the train. At last, the train slowed to a halt just beside a station guard. The doors opened. For a moment Timmy stood quite quite still on the edge of the train. A blast of icy air, sharp as the blade of a knife, cut through him. Suddenly, he didn't want to get off. He felt very, very afraid.

The guard stared downwards, a whistle hung limply from his lips. Timmy swallowed. He knew this man.

'Terminates here, sonny. Hurry along,' he said.

Then he looked up and removed his hat.

Timmy saw his face. With a cry he leapt from the train, rushing past the guard. A pain shot through his body. For a moment he did not know where to turn as confused memories flooded into his head. The platform was deserted. He looked up at the night sky, searching for the moon—but there wasn't one, just a single distant fading star.

There was no sign of his parents. Where was the exit? His breath came in gulps now, like a landed fish. It was getting darker. The few lights in the station were popping out as though someone was switching off the night. He pirouetted. The train was gone, but he had not heard it leave. To his right there was a ticket box, and beside it was a doorway which led to a tunnel. There were no lights but he saw that it did lead somewhere; he hoped out of the station. Making his way slowly into the darkness, his hands barely touched the damp brickwork of the tunnel.

He heard himself moaning softly.

After a moment he was through. His heart felt full with the expectation of perhaps seeing Mummy and Daddy's car. But there was nothing.

Nothing, except for a horse-drawn carriage.

The horse was as black as ebony, almost invisible against the tar coloured air, with a single plume feather sprouting from its bridle. The reins were held by someone Timmy had seen before, several times. An old man with white hair which fell from the sides of a top hat turned towards him and looked down to where he stood.

'Hurry along, sonny,' he said. 'Time to go.'

Then Timmy looked into the face which smiled in a certain sad way, the face he had been avoiding.

Timmy let out a scream, which froze on the air when he caught sight of the coffin that lay in the carriage.

For just a flash he remembered, as if it were a long time ago, somewhere else, somewhere far away. There had been the outline of a person dressed in a hospital gown, hovering above his bed. It was a hazy figure as though in a dream: a kindly doctor whose hair was unusually milky white, who had shaken his head in sorrow and gently touched Timmy's cheek with his hand as he said the words he did not, *could not* understand, '*There is nothing we can do.*'

The single star in the sky went out and the mountains grew all around him. The cold became greater, but with this came a dampness too, a cold earth kind of dampness which ate into his bones as the inky blackness of Timmy's final destination swallowed him whole.

He whispered hoarsely, 'I've arrived.'

First Class

ADÈLE GERAS

Phil was furious. He was livid; incandescent; he went
ballistic. He was whatever the opposite of over the
moon is. Phil is my brother. He's a train buff. We're
all more or less railwayish in my family. My grandad
was a porter. My dad works behind the glass in a ticket
office, and my mum has the best job of all, I reckon.
She pushes one of those trolleys on the Manchester to
Nottingham sprinter train. Up and down the carriages
she goes, in her natty uniform, doling out crisps and
coffee and tea with those silly little milk thingies that
no one can open. KitKats; Mini Cheddars; dry-roasted
peanuts: you name it, she doles it out, with a smile and
a pleasant word.

In between pushing the trolley, she chats with the
driver and the guard. OK, so she's not on the cutting
edge of rail technology or anything, but she's on a train
most of the time. When she's at home, what she likes
doing best is going in for competitions. You know the
sort of thing: making up slogans in fifty words or less
to tell the world why you like this or that cereal or

brand of washing-powder or whatever. She's especially good at rhymes, and always says that it's the soothing rhythm of the train that does it . . . clackety-clack works wonders on your verse, apparently.

Phil, though, is something else. What he doesn't know about trains isn't worth knowing and probably doesn't exist. He learns the big fat railway timetable off by heart. He can tell you the age of every locomotive on the lines today, and also every one that's ended up in a museum. He visits those. He has books and postcards. He sits in a movie and says things like:

'They'd never have had that loco in 1924 . . . (or whenever) . . . it wasn't built till 1935.'

And so forth. Boring, I call it, though it impresses everyone else, and has made Phil a fixture on every school quiz team. It's amazing, apparently, what you pick up about geography and history if you know about TRAINS.

Phil was doing his A-levels in May. That was the real reason for the fury, incandescence, etc. He had his Maths exam on the very day . . . well, I'd better begin at the beginning.

My name is Leonie. I look nothing like a lion. The name is an embarrassment. I look like a pixie who's been on a starvation diet. I am small and skinny and dark. I wish every night that I were taller, plumper, and especially that I had what my horrible brother calls 'VBs'. (I knew you'd ask . . . Viable Boobs.) I know absolutely nothing about trains except for one thing: I love them. I love what they do. I love the way they go through the landscape. I love the way they smell. I think they sound great too. I can fall asleep to the music of their wheels. I like the rocking motion. I like the kind of plastic sandwiches they serve. I think railway stations are terrific. I think what I'm saying is:

I am a fan of JOURNEYS. I like the idea of somewhere else. And trains get you there in the best possible way . . . you can feel time passing. You can read. Listen to music. I even like earwigging other people's conversations on their mobile phones. You can chat to your friends. Snooze. Look out of the window—that's almost the best thing of all, that countryside whooshing past—and then, later on, you're somewhere far away. It's magic.

Once upon a time, then. That's a good way to start a story. Mum went in for a competition once upon a time, only it turned out to be the wrong time. She heard in April that she'd won the TOP PRIZE, but alas and alack for everyone, the date of the Special Treat could not be changed. May 7th it was, and wouldn't you know, that was the same day as the Maths A-level exam. Phil would HAVE to be wrestling with formulae and fretting among the figures, while Mum and I were on our Treat.

'It's not fair,' Phil wailed when he heard. He sounded about six years old and not seventeen.

'Perfectly fair, dear,' said Mum. 'I won. My entry was the best and that was that. You had to agree to abide by the rules of the competition. The date cannot be changed. Your father is working, and you have the exam, so I'm taking Leonie and that's that! We'll have a Girly Day Out. You can go another time. You can get a Student Pass or whatever and take every train you see for the next however many years. This is for us, and I don't want to hear another word about it. We'll bring you back a plastic Eiffel Tower if you're good.'

Phil stomped off to his room, and Mum and I began to discuss exactly what one ought to wear for such a spectacular occasion: a trip on Eurostar, First Class, all the way to Paris and back. All expenses paid.

Mega-double-super BRILLIANT. I could understand how sick poor Phil must be feeling, but quite honestly I was so happy, I found it hard to be sympathetic.

If Phil were telling this, you'd get every single detail about our journey down from Bolton, but he's not, so imagine Mum and me already in London, at Waterloo, going down that escalator into the Eurostar Terminal.

I'll tell you what it's like, if you've never been there. It's like an airport. They've spent a lot of time and money making a railway station look like an airport. You check in, you show people your ticket (and that looks like an air ticket too), and then you sit about in airport-type armchairs and gawp at airport-type shops. Then you go to gates, and file through on to the platform. What's on the platform is a train. What a relief! I was really getting quite nervous, thinking we might all be flying away in a jet. Phil was going to ask me, I knew, so while I didn't take down any numbers or anything nerdish like that, I did notice that it was long and white with stripes along its side, and its nose was smooth and curved. It did look sleek and modern and as if it could go much faster than your normal average train.

When we got to our seats, I spent ages making mine lean back and spring up straight again. You've guessed it: the inside of the train (First Class, anyway . . . I don't know what things were like in Standard!) was just like a plane. Only we had so much room for our feet and in our armchairs that you could probably have fitted another couple of people in, easily. Stewardesses (I don't know if that's what they were called) handed round menus, and free champagne, and later on the lunch was delicious.

'Better than my trolley,' Mum said. 'If I'd been

born a bit later, and was a lot thinner and lived down
south, I'd apply for a job on Eurostar, no question.'

That struck me as an awful lot of 'ifs' but I didn't
say a word. I was too busy scoffing my smashing lunch,
and wondering if there were any seconds of the
chocolates that went with the coffee.

I went to the loo while we were in the Tunnel. That
was the only bit of the journey my mum was a bit
worried about.

'All that water,' she'd said, before we even set out.
'Pressing down on us . . . ' Phil and Dad had tried to
explain, but I knew that Mum wasn't taking it all in.
Neither was I, but I was less worried. I figured they'd
worked it out all right, and that was it. Anyway, I went
to the loo (yes . . . exactly like a plane loo, but loads
bigger) and when I came back, the two seats opposite
us were suddenly taken. They'd been empty before.
Where had these two come from? I hadn't seen them at
Waterloo. Mum had fallen into a doze. It must have
been the champagne. For a moment, I considered
waking her up. Surely you were supposed to enjoy
every single second of your First Prize, and not sleep
the time away? I was just thinking about this when the
man opposite spoke to me:

'It's a disgrace,' he said. He said it to me. He looked
most peculiar. I'd never seen anyone who looked like
that. Partly, he was like an old tramp. He had a long
beard, which seemed . . . no, it couldn't have been
could it? . . . WET. It also struck me as vaguely
greeny-blue. He was wearing a suit of sorts, but it had
a kind of sheen on it. Not lurex exactly, but certainly
shimmery. Too flashy for such an old chap, I thought,
but the girl sitting next to him was so beautiful that I
didn't look at the old man too much. She had long hair
falling right down over her shoulders. A sort of pale,

silvery gold. Silvery gold sounds stupid, but that's the best way I can describe it. And this girl had the bluest eyes I'd ever seen. I decided that she must have been wearing contact lenses. No one's eyes were that blue.

'What is?' I asked. 'What's a disgrace?'

'This is,' he answered. 'This Eurostar.'

I couldn't think what to say. Who could possibly feel Eurostar was a disgrace? And why? I was beginning to get the idea that this man was a nutter. I didn't think you got nutters in First Class, but I was wrong, wasn't I? This was maybe an eccentric millionaire. That was probably what the beautiful girl saw in him . . . his money. He was no beauty. To tell you the truth, he stank of prawns that have gone off a bit. I had just made up my mind to wake my mum and ask her whether we could move to other seats, when he leaned forward and said:

'Listen. No one listens to me. This was my kingdom. No one asked. No one said: please will you give us your Divine Permission to put our land-creature, our metal-and-wood-and-plastic dragon in a tube going right through your territory, did they? No. I'll tell you the truth. They didn't. They came and they used dynamite and they scared the living daylights out of every single thing that swam in my ocean, and then they laid tubes and concrete and now . . . without so much as a by-your-leave . . . there's all this TRAFFIC. It's noisy. It's constant. It shakes the seabed. And no one . . . not one single person . . . has thought to invite me even to have a look, much less offer me any compensation. And my daughter . . . ' (he nodded towards the beautiful girl) ' . . . can't find a place to settle down. Not a rock or a cave anywhere to be found that isn't . . . polluted . . . by this Eurostar creature.'

I didn't know what to say.

'You don't know what to say, do you?' said the man. Could he read minds? How mad was he? I had to wake Mum at once. Or maybe there was a stewardess somewhere? I looked all round the carriage. Everyone was preoccupied. Some had newspapers up in front of their faces. Others were asleep. A couple of people had laptops open on the tables in front of them, and were punching in data and gazing at their little screens in a kind of trance. I felt completely alone, but for this loony and his beautiful and silent companion.

'I think,' I said in the end, 'that this is a wonderful train.'

I felt I had to stick up for Eurostar. Hadn't they just given me and my mum a wonderful treat?

The old man sighed.

'Everyone says that. I haven't found many in sympathy with my views. Never mind. I will . . . we will . . . keep trying. At least we can ensure that no one forgets all about us, eh? You won't forget us, will you, young lady? You'll tell them. Tell them about us. We leave the train here, so I will bid you farewell.'

He stood up, and offered me his hand. The train was travelling at high speed. We were still in the Tunnel. I didn't know much about railways, but I *did* know there wasn't a station until we got out and into France. How was he going to leave the train? I took hold of his hand . . . well, what would you have done? It's rude not to shake hands with someone, isn't it? . . . and it was wet. His hand was wet. And cold. And stinky, like an old fish.

'Goodbye,' he said. 'Please remember the name. Poseidon.'

He and the beautiful girl left their seats and walked up to where the loos were. They went into one loo each. After a bit, the light that said the loos were

engaged went out, so I ran up to see what had happened to them. Neither of them had come back.

There was no one in the loos. Could they have slipped down the plugholes? Impossible. How? I shook my head, trying to understand. Maybe there was a kind of trapdoor in the floor, but I couldn't see one. And what would they do in the Channel Tunnel? It was a mystery. I went back to our seats. I looked at the place where the nutter and the beauty had been sitting. I sniffed. It was still a bit whiffy. I touched the plush. It was definitely damp.

My mum woke up and said, 'Don't know what they put in the champagne. Out like a light, I was. Were you OK?'

'Fine,' I said. 'Mum, have you ever heard of someone called Poseidon?'

'It's another name for Neptune,' she said, fishing in her handbag for her lipstick. 'Greek God of the Sea.'

'He spoke English,' I said. 'The Poseidon I mean.'

My mum looked at me. 'I thought you had orange juice instead of champagne . . . whatever are you talking about?'

'Nothing. It's OK,' I said. But I thought about the nutter all day, while we were in Paris, and I watched out for him and his beautiful companion on the way back, when we went through the Tunnel. I looked out of the window all the way from France to England, for the whole twenty minutes, and I don't think I saw anyone. Or maybe I did. Maybe there was an old man waving at me in the dark: a wild-bearded old man, with a shimmery suit, waving and waving in the blackness at the lighted Eurostar dragon flying through the depths of the ocean. Maybe. I can't be sure.

A Puff of Steam

WILLIAM MAYNE

Mel, Joe, and Kev were walking along the alley at the back of a row of houses. It was a Sunday morning and there was not much to do. Mel was talking about a group called The Immortals, Joe was talking about ways of cooking cabbage, and Kev was talking about being a truckie with his own unit, one of these days.

They went up as far as the middle of the alley and passed a big lillypilly tree. When it was behind them Mel said something.

He said, 'Go on talking but listen to me and don't turn your heads.'

'Are you trying a trick on us?' said Kev.

'No,' said Mel. 'Listen. You know Dee.'

They knew Dee. Dee was a boy who wanted to join them and go with them. But they thought he was useless and did not want him.

'He's up in that tree listening to us,' said Mel. 'Don't look round. What'll we do?'

'Leave him there,' said Kev. 'Saw off the bottom of the tree so he can't get down.'

But no one understood that. You can't do it.

'Look,' said Joe, 'we'll have to tell him straight that we don't want him. We'll turn round, walk to the bottom of the tree, climb in it with him and tell him to get lost forever.'

So they swung around and marched back to the tree and went up into it as fast as they could.

Dee was sitting in the top. He could tell what they meant to say by the way they looked at him.

'I'm not following you,' he said.

'Yeah?' said Kev. 'But you're here, aren't you?'

'It's more like you followed me,' said Dee.

'Only up in the tree,' said Joe. 'You know why.'

'Look,' said Dee, 'I kind of took the hint the other day. I'm not following you. I just came up the alley on my way to my grandad's house, and you came up the alley at the other end, so I got up the tree out of the way.'

Mel said, 'Let's leave him. You can't prove anything with someone like him.'

'My uncle lives just over the fence,' said Dee. 'This is just where he is. It's true what I say. See down there,' and he pointed down the other side of the fence of the alley.

'It's a creek or something,' said Joe. 'We don't believe you, Dee.'

'You go down there,' said Dee, 'and I'll go round to my grandad's house and come through the door and show you what he's got.'

'Great,' said Mel. 'Any of you guys want to see what his grandad's got?'

'No way,' said Joe and Kev. 'Not him or his grandad, ever.'

'Good,' said Dee. 'I shouldn't have said anything about it.'

So that seemed to be all. The three of them climbed down the tree again and went down the alley. Dee climbed down after them and went the other way. They watched him go.

'I wonder what his grandad's got?' said Mel.

'I didn't know there was a creek down there,' said Joe.

'We'd better find out about both things,' said Kev.

So they went back to the tree and over the fence into a patch of bush. They thought it was the bank of a creek and went down to the bottom. But at the bottom there was a rusty railway line, not a creek. Rusty, with trees beginning to grow up through it. No trains came along here.

If the train isn't coming there's no point in standing by the track. So they walked along it. It went along the cutting and then stopped.

They thought it went against a fence, but when they looked again they saw that the rusty rails ran under a pair of big doors.

'Back of the station,' said Mel. 'But it can't be. The station's over the other way.'

'Tell you what,' said Joe, 'it's a factory line, there'll be a factory the other side, that's what.'

But in a moment or two it seemed unlikely there was a factory beyond, because they heard Dee's voice the other side of the door.

Railway lines. A closed door. Dee's voice. Dee's grandad with something interesting.

'You know what I think,' said Mel.

'Yeah,' said Kev. 'But you're stupid.'

'He can't have,' said Joe.

But no one was going to stand out and say what they thought was beyond the door.

'One way to find out,' said Joe. And he knocked on it with his fist.

'That's them,' said Dee's voice the other side. 'Grandad, they came, let them in.'

'He'll get a surprise if it isn't us,' said Joe.

'But it is us,' said Kev. 'Aren't you?'

There was a rattling of bolts and clicking of keys and the sliding of bars. The doors shook, and then one of them pushed itself open. Or Dee and his grandad pushed it.

There was a railway engine beyond the door, in a big shed. It was a steam engine. It was very old and made a long time ago. It was very clean and bright so that it looked new as well.

'It's mine,' said Dee's grandad. 'It's a Stephenson single-wheeler that used to belong to the State railway, and then was sold to Iramoo Implements Industries, I.I.I. They sold the driver with it, and we retired together and here we are. We sometimes have a run up and down the track here. I was just thinking of firing up and we'll go tonight.'

'Oh,' said Mel, 'what's it like being sold?'

'Like getting married again,' said the old man. 'It's the only way of keeping the job going.'

'He's a bachelor,' said Joe.

'He hasn't lived,' said the old man. 'Now, you want a ride, you bring some coal or those nasty briquettes or we shan't have a blaze. Did you tell your friends that, Dee?'

It was one thing to look at the engine for an hour. That was good and interesting, but didn't last forever. But it was another matter if people were going to think they were Dee's friend. If anything Dee might be their friend, but they were not even going to let that happen.

So they looked, and then Mel thought it was lunch

time, and they went away again without promising any coal or briquettes. Bringing anything like that would make Dee the friend of the group, and they knew that was impossible.

They went home and had lunch. 'I can't come out after,' said Mel. 'My dad and I got some work to do.'

'Got to go see my auntie,' said Kev.

'That's OK,' said Joe. 'See you tomorrow.'

But Mel had decided he would go back with some fuel for the engine and have a ride on it. After lunch he took four of the plastic packs of briquettes and humped them to the alley, under the tree, over the fence, and along the cutting.

He saw that Dee had already been bringing some, because there was a small stack outside the doors.

He was wrong. It was Joe that opened the door.

'It's like this,' said Mel. 'Well, I thought if I came alone we wouldn't have to have him in with us.'

'I thought the same,' said Joe. 'But let's kill Kev when he comes, telling lies about his auntie.'

So they jumped Kev when he came and no one minded that much.

After that there was a lot to be done. Mr Olanik, Dee's grandad, had them polishing and greasing and carrying water and getting hotter and hotter and more and more dirty themselves. The fire in the engine was lit, but the engine was in the shed so the smoke had nowhere to go, and the heat had no escape. He had them walking down the track as well, cutting down the small trees that had grown up in the last year. The engine had not been out for that time.

The trip, when it came, took about ten minutes, longer than Mr Olanik meant to take. First there came a moment when he pulled a lever and they heard steam

crack its way along a pipe and then stand for a short
time without doing anything.

Then there was a sort of a small shake in the
engine, and from the wheels there came a noise like
sugar being trodden on, which was the rust on the
rails being powdered. From the engine itself came a
puffing roar and there was movement, and then there
was going.

Slowly they went down the length of the cutting,
past the lillypilly tree, out to where the cutting opened
out and there was a wire fence ahead, with the rails
going under it and into the goods yard and the
workshops of the State railway.

'This is how far we go,' said Mr Olanik. He stopped
the engine and had another tube of beer. He had a pack
with him, because he had worked hardest, and was
hottest.

'We go back now,' he said. They slid back into the
cover of the cutting.

'Not very far,' said Dee.

'Not far enough,' said Mr Olanik. The engine went
backwards as far as the lillypilly tree and stopped. 'Not
far enough,' he said again.

And then they were moving forwards again, and this
time they did not stop at the end of the cutting but
went further.

'No one about Sunday,' said Mr Olanik, and they
did not stop at the fence but went through it and they
were on the State railway line.

'Well, this is too far now,' said Mr Olanik, peering
ahead. 'We go one way we crash into a truck. We go
the other we come off the rails at the points. We get
our best choice and go home again. But first, I show
them I'm here.'

His way of showing he was here was to blow the

whistle of the engine three times, and then put the lever over to reverse and take them back the way they had come. They went through the broken fence, into the cutting, and stopped.

'Look what some foolish person done to the fence,' said Mr Olanik. 'Must have been a cow on the line, did you see a cow, charging about?'

'Yeah, big mob,' said Kev.

'They don't let me drive on their lines, I send my cows through their fence,' said Mr Olanik. 'Now we better go home or they see us.'

So they went back, slower and slower, because there was not much steam left. Then it was tea time, and their visit was over.

The next few days they expected trouble from Dee. He was bound to be a pest to them. But he was not. He stayed away, not bothering them at all.

'He isn't so bad,' said Joe.

'He's just getting at you by being nice,' said Kev.

'Don't think about him,' said Mel. 'He doesn't come anywhere near.'

But next Sunday it was the three of them that loitered near the lillypilly tree, in case things began to happen anywhere along the cutting.

Nothing happened. In the end they went down to the rails and walked up to the doors. But all was quiet there, and no one answered their tap on the wood.

And at the State railway end of the cutting they found the wire fence up again. And the rails that ran under it were lifted from their bed and laid to one side.

Mr Olanik had showed the railway something with his whistle. And they had shown him something back. He couldn't easily get out on their roads again.

'Well, poor old guy,' said Joe.

'Can't even take his wife out for a drive on Sunday now,' said Kev. It wasn't exact sense, but the meaning was clear.

Grease Monkey Jack—the Engineer

ROBERT DAWSON

Mum bundled a brown paper package into my hand. I unwrapped one corner, just to check . . .

'Bread and cheese for your snap. I'm so proud of you, Jack.'

She flung her arms round me.

'Aw, Mum.'

Other people were also setting off for work, mostly, like me, in the railway yards. For me it was different. Yesterday, I had reached the grand old age of 13: today, 31 December 1899, I was starting work.

'Here,' Mum said, thrusting something into my hand. 'Your Uncle Aaron wanted you to have his silver pocket watch. He says even grease monkeys need to know the time,' she smiled.

I slipped the end of the chain through a waistcoat button hole and tucked it into a pocket.

'Good luck, Jack,' she called, as my heavy boots clumped down the street, smashing the ice puddles in the gutters. My father worked in the yards until

he died. He was a good engineer, quickly able to find any fault in engines. His good name had got me the job.

Noise surrounded me as I entered through the yard's huge gates. I swallowed hard and half wished I was 12 again. I saw a man in a dark suit who seemed to be in charge.

'Excuse me, sir,' I called.

'This isn't a place for boys,' he shouted. 'It's dangerous. Out!' and pointed towards the great gates.

'No, sir, you don't understand. It's my first day and I was told to report to Trafalgar Wilkes.'

'Mr Wilkes to you. He's a most respected man here. You will find him . . . no, wait. Oi, you!' he called to a youth. 'Take this boy to Mr Wilkes, and don't let him get squashed.'

'Thank you, sir,' I said. I touched Mum's reassuring snap packet.

The youth strode towards a long shed in the distance.

'Do you work here?' I asked.

'Don't speak to me: don't you know who I am, boy?' he snapped.

Who was he, only a couple of years older, to talk like that and call me boy as well?

'No,' I said simply, though I felt like saying much more.

'I'm a fireman,' he said. 'And we're special. Next I'll be an engine driver. The cream! And you, boy, are only a grease monkey, I'll be bound.'

My dad had explained it. Everyone wanted to drive engines. Even my father had never managed that. You needed to know someone important. I knew none of the shareholders in the railway, or the managers, so I had no chance.

We entered the shed. Several engines, their boilers out, were there.

'That's Mr Wilkes, over there, boy,' he said. He pointed to a tall man, slim, but with obvious strength, directing some men as they lifted a wheel off an engine. As the young fireman walked off, I noticed how his shoes shone. I approached Mr Wilkes.

I remembered my manners. 'Excuse me, Mr Wilkes, I'm . . . '

That's as far as I got. 'Jack, isn't it? You've got your father's face. If you're half as good, we shan't fall out. Take a rag,' he pointed, 'and polish all the brasswork up on that engine. And shut your mouth before it fills with grease and get on with it until I have time to come to you,' Mr Wilkes growled.

'Right, Mr Wilkes.'

'And call me sir,' he said, resuming work.

I wandered over to the engine, scrambled up on to the ledge at the bottom of the boiler and began half-heartedly wiping down the boiler pipes. I couldn't resist a look underneath. I saw the great iron wheels, the enormous pistons and the connecting rod—the pressure of the piston forced one wheel to turn, and the connecting rod pushed the next wheel. This wasn't a huge engine, with only four wheels in the middle and no extra bogies.

As I gazed at the wonders of modern engineering, I noticed that one of the wheels looked absolutely dry where the axle went through. I knew it shouldn't. I found a grease can, crawled underneath and carefully greased the dry part.

'Well, Jack,' called a voice. 'You're your father's son right enough.'

I crawled out to meet Mr Wilkes's boots.

'Yes, sir,' I said, 'I saw a dry spot and . . . '

'I can see, boy. Someone shouldn't have missed that.
I don't think much of your polishing, but you
obviously have your father's feel for machinery. Now
listen, boy. One of the drivers has slipped on ice and
broken his leg. They're a driver short. It's only a local
run, and they've asked me.'

He must have seen my look of amazement. 'I was a
driver for many years, but good engineers are hard to
find and I'm a good one of those too. You can go with
me.'

I nearly fell over with surprise and delight.

'But, Jack, the fireman is your senior. You must call
him Mister. And you'll help stoke the firebox when he
tells you. It'll be a hard day's work.'

'Right, sir,' I said.

'Now come, boy, and close that mouth.'

I trotted proudly behind him. 'Where are we going,
sir?' I asked.

'Derby to Buxton, stopping at every station on the
way. Four coaches and Mr Silverdyke in one. You'd
best be on good behaviour.'

'Who, sir?'

'Why, Jack, don't you know? Mr Silverdyke's one of
the company's main shareholders. He's off to Buxton to
take the waters. Buxton water's good for you, so he'll
stay in a hotel and drink it to clean out his system.'

The engine was already stoked up. It was larger than
the one I'd been polishing, a 0-4-2 with two extra
smaller wheels at the back. Its chimney was almost as
tall as me. Mr Wilkes clambered up onto the platform.
I could hear someone in the cab, shovelling.

I climbed in, and was surprised that the shovelling
fireman was the youth who'd been sent with me to find
Mr Wilkes.

'Oh,' said Mr Wilkes, at the same moment as my

heart sank. 'This is Albert Castle, the yard manager's nephew.' I could tell that Mr Wilkes didn't approve.

'Oh,' repeated Albert Castle when he saw me. 'It's the grease monkey. Don't get in my way, boy.'

'And don't you get in mine,' said Mr Wilkes, pushing Albert to one side as he checked a dial.

Then we were off, chugging slowly backwards into Derby station. I leaned out of the cab into the frosty air, feeling important.

Then I saw a tall figure striding along the platform, with the station master alongside. I guessed this was Mr Silverdyke. He wore a black overcoat, black top hat, black suit—and his shoes shone like diamonds.

I jumped down from the cab to get a closer look. He had thin gold pince-nez glasses clipped to the end of his nose, which was long and hooked like an eagle's. But his eyes were kind, with smile-lines radiating from their corners.

'Get back in this cab!'

Mr Wilkes sounded cross, but I didn't understand. 'Sir?'

'Your shoes. It's a company rule to look smart and have polished shoes and your boots—well,' he gasped.

I felt like a criminal. My boots were so dull and scuffed alongside Albert's and Mr Wilkes's. I didn't understand why even a fireman shovelling coal had to have shining shoes, let alone a grease monkey like me.

I rubbed one boot against the back of my breeches, then the other, to try to make them look a little better. It didn't seem to help.

Mr Wilkes turned the handle and we were away, chugging, slowly out of the station.

Tsi tsi tsi.

It was such a happy sound, and as we gathered speed I forgot the problem over the boots. Time

seemed to stand still. I reached inside my waistcoat to
feel Uncle Aaron's watch.

Albert's face glowed red with the exertion of the
shovelling and the heat of the fire.

'Get shovelling, boy, or are you a first class
passenger like Mr Silverdyke?'

I looked at Mr Wilkes, but he was too busy
watching the track and the signalling to notice. A
shovel hung near the firebox. It wasn't rusty like
Albert's but had a peculiar sheen varying between
copper and grey-blue. I lifted it off its hook.

'No!' Mr Wilkes had shouted at me again. 'Not that
shovel. That's a special one.'

He pointed to a battered, bent, and very rusty
one.

The old shovel was awkward. It didn't take the coal
cleanly, and I only managed a few nuggets on it. I
turned and, as I had seen Albert do, threw the coal at
the firebox.

I missed, and all the coal fell onto the cab floor in
front of the box.

'We want it in the firebox, foolish boy,' Albert
leered.

I felt stupid. I leaned forward, took the pieces in my
hands, and threw them one at a time into the fire. The
heat felt as if it would sear my face.

'Here, like this.' Mr Wilkes took the shovel from
me. He used it easily as if it had been a teaspoon. He
scooped a heap of coal and threw without even taking a
step towards the fire. Every single piece went in, and to
the back. 'Look at the angle,' he said.

I saw how the shovel was slightly up in the air.
Then he threw again and all but one of the nuggets
flew into the firebox.

'Now you try,' he said.

Albert stood to one side, sniggering. Mr Wilkes glared at him but said nothing.

I shovelled and threw. Less than half landed in the firebox with my first shovel, and all but two cobbles on the fifth. I was getting the hang of it.

'Now I must get us into the station,' said Mr Wilkes, and he slowed the train just in time to arrive at Duffield station.

Moments later we were on our way again. The rhythm of the engine was as regular as a song, tsi, tsi, tsi, tsi and occasionally a pattern of six tsis. I was so proud.

After Ambergate, Mr Wilkes ordered, 'Get shovelling, Jack, this is a difficult stretch of line. It's uphill all the way now. Up, up, and up again. And after Whatstandwell there's one of the longest hill tunnels on the line—half a mile on a bad gradient. We need all the steam we can get. Shovel as if the devil himself was behind us!'

I did, priding myself on my new-found ability to throw all the coal onto the fire (well, nearly all), but, as Mr Wilkes had said, as if my life depended on it.

Albert was already heaving and throwing as fast as he could, sweat pouring down his face.

At first all went well, but as we approached the infamous Cromford tunnel, I heard the noise of the motion change. It became tish-ta-warr, tish-ta-warr. We were in the tunnel itself when something caused the wheels to lose their grips. Suddenly, they spun round—clclclclclcl.

'Sand!' Mr Wilkes shouted. Albert leaped to one side of the cab. I saw him pull a handle at the side and heard a rush of steam.

'No! No! No!' Mr Wilkes was screaming. I did not understand why. 'Wait, wait!'

The wheels spun again, I heard an ominous thud, and then they were gripping once more.

But by now the train had lost almost all its speed. We crawled out of the tunnel and into Cromford.

Mr Wilkes rounded on Albert. 'You fool! You're supposed to know. You never release sand for the wheels to seize when they're actually spinning. The strain—it can snap pistons or even the wheels!'

Albert shrugged. 'It hasn't done any harm.'

'Huh. If it has, you can explain it personally to Mr Silverdyke. But we shall see.'

From then on, Mr Wilkes kept leaning from the cab and listening to the sound of the wheels.

After the massive viaduct at Monsal Dale, we entered a long tunnel hacked through solid rock. The engine resumed its tish-ta-warr, tish-ta-warr rhythm. We were all-but emerging from the tunnel when there was a crash from somewhere alongside the engine. Mr Wilkes rushed to that side of the cab. The engine power dropped rapidly. It slid, more than drove, over the top of the incline, the wheels obviously no longer gripping, and stopped. Mr Wilkes slammed on the brakes to prevent us slipping back.

Mr Wilkes leaped down and gazed at the wheels. Albert and I followed.

I saw the problem instantly. The connecting rod between the wheels had fallen off so that no power could get to the wheels to make them turn. But the rod seemed undamaged.

'Now what's to do?' Mr Wilkes groaned. I slipped between two wheels to get a better view.

'The bolts have sheered,' I told him. He put his fingers against the remains of the bolts, each the thickness of a man's wrist.

'Snapped,' he agreed. 'That sand, I knew we would have to pay for the mistake.'

'It wasn't my fault,' Albert whined.

'It's your error, and yours entirely. Tell your uncle that tonight, if we're home by then. And meanwhile, warn the signal box.' He pointed through the tunnel. 'Quickly, before Mr Silverdyke comes,' he added.

Albert needed no second bidding, and ran.

Now, I looked more closely at the bolts. One was hanging out and I slipped it into my pocket. The other two were jammed in by years of dirt and grime. If only I could find three more bolts, and the right tools, I realized I could mend it.

'There's no danger of other trains behind us on this single track,' Mr Wilkes said. 'They'll send another engine to complete the journey and shunt us to a repair shed.'

'What's to do?' a voice asked. I looked out from under the engine and saw it was Mr Silverdyke. 'Mr Wilkes isn't it?'

'Yes, sir,' said the driver. He tucked out from under the wheels and stood. He explained the problem.

'From the skidding, I expect?' Mr Silverdyke asked, but Mr Wilkes didn't reply.

'I've sent the fireman to the signal box,' said Mr Wilkes. 'This boy is a grease monkey, Herbert Smith's son.'

'Yes, Mr Wilkes, I remember him. A fine man. Here for the ride, eh, boy?'

'Yes, sir, my first day's work, sir.'

'Good, good,' Mr Silverdyke murmured. He peered under the engine. 'It looks a simple repair. We're close to Miller's Dale. Surely there's a blacksmith there.'

My hand went involuntarily towards Uncle Aaron's watch. I remembered immediately.

'My Uncle Aaron, sir,' I said. 'He *is* the blacksmith at Miller's Dale. Shall I run there, sir, and see if he can help?'

'Yes, yes,' Mr Silverdyke agreed. 'As fast as you can.'

I'm sure I ran every bit as quickly as Albert. It was about two miles to Miller's Dale, and I was there in less than fifteen minutes.

But when I reached the smithy, Uncle Aaron wasn't there. I explained to Aunt Tilly, snatched a large hammer, metal punches, spanners, and heavy bolts, the same thickness as the one I had brought.

By the time I reached the engine, an hour had passed. Albert had already returned.

I felt very important as I crawled under. I put a punch at one of the broken bolts and began to hammer. Soon, the bolt was out. I put a new one in, and started on the second bolt.

A few strikes of the hammer against the metal punch and it had slumped to the sleepers, too.

Then Mr Wilkes, Albert, and I picked up the connecting rod. My heart was in my mouth in case it had, in fact, been damaged, but it slipped onto the bolts like butter on toast.

I took the split pins and tapped them until they were secure, and this time, Albert helped too.

'Well done, Jack Smith,' said Mr Silverdyke, as the guard sheep-dogged the other passengers back onto the train.

From then on, Mr Wilkes insisted on taking the train steadily, but we made Miller's Dale with no problem. Aunt Tilly was there, and as we pulled out again, I saw Uncle Aaron on a bridge, waving frantically, his face almost cut in half by a great grin. I waved back and tapped my waistcoat so he would know I had his watch safe.

As we tsi-tsied along, Mr Wilkes suddenly said, 'You did well there, Jack, and you have made your mark with Mr Silverdyke. It's time to celebrate with a late breakfast.'

He took the oddly coloured shovel and spread thick bacon rashers on it. 'Get your snap ready, boys.' He pushed the shovel into the firebox and immediately withdrew it. The bacon was done to a turn, and I understood immediately—that shovel was the frying pan!

Albert and I wrapped our chunks of bread round the rashers and munched happily.

Buxton was the end of our out journey. A replacement engine was brought so that they could do a more permanent repair on our 0-4-2. Mr Silverdyke came up to me.

Self-consciously, I rubbed my shoes on the back of my trousers.

'You did a good job there,' he said. 'I shall remember you for the future. You're a boy who understands engines.'

'Thank you sir.'

I glowed with pride.

Then Mr Wilkes's voice brought me back to reality. 'Come along, Jack Smith, our new engine's here. It's down hill nearly all the way this time! So you can enjoy the journey while Mr Castle keeps up the steam.'

'Yes, sir.' I clambered into the cab, and we were off.

The rest is history. But even years later, when I drove the Royal Scot itself, there was no one more proud of my start to the century. In one day I'd become Grease Monkey Jack—the engineer-fireman.

Penalty For Improper Use

HILARY McKAY

PENALTY FOR IMPROPER USE: TWENTY-FIVE POUNDS

Those were the first words that Rupert learnt to read. They were written in large black letters above the communication cord. The communication cord stopped the train.

It was not really a cord at all, but a red, plasticky looking handle, high up above a window, right near the roof of the carriage. Rupert was eight years old before he could reach it. Even then he had to stand on a seat and lean right over and he could only just touch it with the tip of one finger.

Even touching it with one finger seemed an amazing thing to Rupert. Until he was eight he had only been able to stare at it. He had stared at it twice a day, five times a week, forty weeks a year for three years.

Rupert's full name was Rupert Lionus Quibelle Darling. When he was born various kind and brave

people had hinted to his mother that this might be a hard name for a boy to live with all his life. She had bent to kiss the baby, smiled, and replied, 'I changed my mind over and over. It was either that, or Lancelot Merlin.'

This information made the kind and brave people think that Rupert had escaped quite lightly. They quickly talked of something else, in case his mother should change her mind again. Rupert's father had nothing to say in the matter. He left the family home shortly after his son learnt to talk, and neither Rupert or his mother ever thought of him again.

What Rupert mostly talked about was trains, but by the time he was six and had started school his interest in trains had more or less concentrated onto one particular thing. The communication cord.

Rupert went to school in the little town two stops down the line from the village where he lived. The station was right next to his house, and so it was only natural that he should travel to school by train. Trains rumbled past the end of his garden, and rumbled through his dreams at night. Even in his sleep Rupert was aware of the unpulled communication cords passing by him.

At school Rupert did very well indeed. His work was never less than very good, and often startlingly perfect. Some teachers liked him very much, and the ones who didn't could never find anything worse than 'Lacks a Sense of Humour' to put on his reports. His name, which would have nearly destroyed some children, gave him no problems at all. From the very beginning Rupert had been hardly aware of the people around him, and he cared nothing for what they thought. Probably he could have survived being named Lancelot Merlin after all. He was absolutely waterproof

when it came to teasing, and he was quite popular too, in a strange sort of way. There was nothing in his life to stop him being completely happy, except that it had been very clearly explained to him that he could not pull the communication cord.

'Except in dire emergency,' said his mother, 'and don't you forget it!'

Rupert did not forget it.

'I could pull it in a dire emergency,' he said to the ticket collector.

'It would have to be dire,' said the ticket collector who knew Rupert well and did not trust him at all. 'Make no mistake! They would slap that fine on you soon as look at you. Twenty-five pounds.'

In those days twenty-five pounds was an awful lot of money. You could buy a new bike for twenty-five pounds. The Railway Authorities obviously thought that the threat of losing so much would make even the most hardened practical joker think again. The Railway Authorities must have been right, because although Rupert asked, he could never discover anyone who had pulled the communication cord. No one had even heard of such a thing happening. He tried to talk about it to the boys at school, but they hooted with laughter and refused to take the idea seriously. Some of them said it was impossible. You just couldn't pull it. It would not pull. Some of them said that Rupert was mad.

Rupert was about eight and a half years old when it dawned on him that if he wanted to pull the communication cord all he had to do was to save up twenty-five pounds.

Something in Rupert's mind seemed to relax after that. He gave up staring quite so hard at the communication cord and he no longer bothered the ticket collectors with his alarming questions. In return

they stopped treating him like an unexploded bomb, and began smiling at him when they took his fare. Rupert smiled happily back. He was saving up his twenty-five pounds.

At Christmas and on his birthday he asked for money instead of presents. He saved every penny of his pocket money, and as much school dinner money as he could get away with. Mother's Day, and other expensive occasions passed safely and economically. His mother was touched and delighted at the amount of time he spent concocting homemade cards, paper flowers, and dressing table ornaments made out of washing up bottles, toilet roll middles, and sticky back plastic

At school a boy lost his tie and Rupert took off his own and sold it to him. Soon afterwards there were a number of mysterious disappearances of things like school jumpers (with the school crest on them), football socks, rulers, and pens. This caused very little upset because Rupert was always willing to come forward at once, with offers of replacements. He charged very little: pocket money prices. No one really minded losing their belongings when they could buy a much cleaner, newer substitute from Rupert for a fraction of the price in the shops. Besides, the lost articles always turned up sooner or later (Rupert was very good at finding things too). The only person who was seriously annoyed was Rupert's mother.

'I don't know what Rupert does with his school things these days,' she complained to another mother she happened to meet in the town.

'All boys lose things,' said the other mother, and turned away. She didn't like Rupert. He had been to a party at their house only the week before, and had won the Pass The Parcel and asked very politely for cash instead.

Rupert's savings were all in coins, fifty pences, and twenties, lots of pennies. Every time he got together five pounds worth he would take it to the post office and get it swapped for a five pound note. He kept the five pound notes in an envelope which he pinned to the inside of his vest. It took him just under a year to save up the twenty-five pounds.

No sooner had he saved it than an astonishing thing happened. His mother took him shopping in the nearest big city. They didn't go on one of the little three carriage trains that Rupert travelled to school on, but a much bigger, much smarter one. Rupert had never been on such a train before and he looked at once for the communication cord and saw to his absolute astonishment the same familiar words.

PENALTY FOR IMPROPER USE: TWENTY-FIVE POUNDS

Crikey, thought Rupert, which was not a word he had ever used before. Crikey. The same price. What a bargain!

It shook him so much that he did not pull the communication cord, although he had the money safely pinned next to his heart and could have done it whenever he wanted. What stopped him was the thought that there might be even bigger trains that he could afford to stop. And there were. As soon as he could he slipped away from his mother at the city station and discovered them for himself. Huge InterCity expresses, endless carriages long, snaking right down their platforms and out of the station. After a bit of running and dodging he managed to climb aboard a stationary one and locate the communication cord. A moment later his frantic mother caught up with him and pulled him off. It did not matter because he had read the warning notice by then. Twenty-five pounds. More than a bargain, this time. A gift.

'Can we go to London?' he asked breathlessly. 'When can we go to London on an InterCity express?'

His mother did not say when. She was very angry. Very, very angry, especially as Rupert was looking as if he had discovered buried treasure. She said, 'There'll be no shopping for you today! I'm taking you straight back home!'

Rupert, who had golden brown curls and shining blue eyes, smiled gloriously up at her, and she saw that he could not care less.

'And don't imagine I will ever bring you with me again!' she said.

She was so furious that Rupert thought she really might mean what she said and was slightly alarmed. And as time went on he grew more and more alarmed, because it seemed to be true. There were no more shopping trips. Worse still, she seemed to go deaf at the mention of visits to London on an InterCity express. He begged and pleaded and pestered and sulked but she took no notice. Poor Rupert was back on the little branch line train again with twenty-five pounds, in five pound notes, burning to be spent.

After a while it began to feel to Rupert as if he had been waiting all his life, which he had, in a way. He began to think that after all it might be better to begin with a small, familiar train, and then work up to an InterCity express.

'I can always save up another twenty-five pounds,' said Rupert, and on his tenth birthday, as an extra special present to himself, he unpinned the twenty-five pounds from the inside of his vest and put it in his pocket instead.

It was a perfect day for it; a wild wind and pouring rain. Perhaps we'll skid, thought Rupert happily.

He was allowed to travel to school alone these days, and he was much taller too. On the morning of his birthday the carriage was nearly empty. He waited for his favourite bit of track; the long curving stretch that swung into the tunnel.

The communication cord was so hard to pull that he had to swing with both feet off the ground, and he wrenched his shoulder. For a second he thought it had not worked, and then there was a bone-crunching lurch and he was flung to his knees. The wheels screamed on the track. Glass shattered, wailing began to come from all around, and Rupert saw white and gold stars, flying and circling around his head. Louder than all the other sounds he heard a voice. Bellowing.

'Penalty for improper use!' bellowed the voice, as close to Rupert as a mouth in his ear, and the stars whizzed even faster around his head.

Sick and shaking, but light-headed with happiness, Rupert gripped the five pound notes in his pocket, ready for the moment when he would have to pay the price.

The moment did not come. Despite the broken glass, the fear, the cuts and blood, even despite the old man who had a heart attack shortly afterwards. Instead Rupert was a hero. A local hero anyway.

RAILWAY CHILD SAVES OUR TRAIN

ran the headline in the local paper, because the train had stopped just inside the mouth of the tunnel, and a

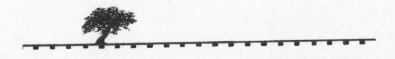

metre in front (at most) was a huge pile of fallen earth and stone. The roof of the tunnel, in fact, had tumbled down.

'How did you know?' they asked him, first the ticket collector, pale as a boiled cauliflower, and then all the others, dozens and dozens, who heard the story.

'I just did,' said Rupert, and they shook their heads and stared at him, and said perhaps he'd somehow caught a glimpse. Subconsciously. Miraculously.

'Yes,' agreed Rupert happily, and hugged his twenty-five pounds tight against his chest.

I didn't have to pay! he rejoiced. I can do it again!

His chance came almost at once. His mother had been almost washed away with pride when she read the article beginning, *Local youngster, Rupert Lionus Quibelle Darling* . . . It seemed to make her forget she had said she would not take him shopping in the city again. She took him the very next week. Or would have taken him, if Rupert, almost weeping with excitement, had not leapt to his feet and run the length of the carriage and pulled the communication cord as soon as the ticket collector's back had turned.

There was the same horrible lurch. The same fearful wailing from passengers. The same scream of brakes and clatter of noise. The same streams of blood from smashed-in noses as people fell forwards. Someone in the carriage began groaning, great rattling groans. Rupert saw the same bright stars again and he heard the voice too, but this time screeching. Still, the same words.

The difference was that this time there was no blocked tunnel to save him.

He only got away with it because of who he was, Rupert Lionus Quibelle Darling, the Railway Child who had saved the train only a week before.

'Do you *know* what the penalty for improper use is?' demanded the Station Police.

Rupert pulled out his twenty-five pounds.

Delayed shock, wrote Rupert's doctor in an explanatory letter to the Station Police. Rupert could not explain it at all.

'Delayed shock,' Rupert's mother told people thankfully, 'and after all, nobody died!'

'This time!' said people. 'Old lady ended up in hospital though. They say she'll never be the same again.'

'Oh well,' said Rupert's mother uncomfortably, and arranged that in future Rupert should go to school by bus.

'He's jinxed,' they began to say at school. 'Rupert's jinxed. He's mad. Catch me on a train with Rupert!'

Even a year later, when there was a school trip to London on an InterCity express they remembered. No one signed up for it at all, except Rupert of course. There was his name, all alone at the top of the list pinned outside the staffroom door.

'Jinxed,' they told a new boy who might otherwise have signed. 'Twice he's been on trains and pulled the communication cord! Twice there's been accidents! Once someone nearly died and once someone did die!'

Rupert could hardly bear it. He begged people. 'Sign up quick, before they take the notice down!'

'You've got to be joking!' they said, and the notice did come down.

'Fools!' said Rupert, clutching his envelope of five pound notes.

That was when Rupert was eleven. When he was twelve he went to Secondary School and things got better. He was put into Class 7b where they were all new together. Only a few boys had come up with him from his old school and, like everyone else, they were much too busy and bewildered to remember things that had happened years ago, when they were only ten.

The day came at last when Rupert found himself on an InterCity express, rushing down to London at a hundred miles an hour to visit the Science Museum.

He got his twenty-five pounds ready, everyone saw it. He sauntered along the carriage, almost casually, like someone going down to buy a drink perhaps, or to speak to a friend.

'Don't drop that money, love!' said a woman kindly as he passed.

Rupert pulled the communication cord with the ease of a lifetime's practice. The whole carriage saw him. The whole carriage heard his terrible wail. For a brief moment he saw the stars again, and then he saw nothing at all.

'What was it he shouted?' people asked. 'Poor boy! Poor boy! What was it he shouted?'

'He shouted, "*Penalty for Improper Use!*"' said a boy. It was Martin, the same boy who had invited Rupert to his party, long ago. '"*Penalty for Improper Use!*" Like that! And he held out a handful of money. And then the train stopped and Rupert fell down and by the time someone reached him the money was gone. That was queer, how the money was gone. There was nobody near him to take it.'

'Poor boy! Poor boy!' said the woman who had warned Rupert not to drop his money on his way down the carriage.

At the next station Class 7b looked out of the window and saw Rupert, now a neat, red blanketed parcel, being lifted out of the guard's van.

'Where will they take him?' wondered everyone.

Large blue notices over different doorways offered not quite suitable alternatives.

WAITING, REFRESHMENTS, STRICTLY PRIVATE, and **LEFT LUGGAGE**.

However Rupert was carried unhesitatingly through a cavernous archway labelled **WAY OUT** which seemed just right.

And then the train went on to London and Class 7b visited the Science Museum as planned.

'Better than going home and brooding,' said one of the teachers who was taking the trip.

No one brooded at all, in fact once they reached London, no one gave Rupert another thought until the journey home. By that time they were all so tired that the events of the morning seemed a long time ago.

'At least there was nobody hurt this time,' remarked Martin, yawning a little. 'Nobody killed.'

'No,' agreed his neighbour. 'Well, Rupert, I suppose.'

'Oh yes, of course,' agreed Martin, slightly guiltily.

'He had a funny name.'

'I know. I used to know it once.'

Martin struggled for a few moments to remember, and then gave up.

By the time they arrived home they had nearly forgotten Rupert.

Soon they would forget him completely.

Dust

JOHN GORDON

Things were going wrong. Sam's father was under the table—again. And his mother once more poked her head up through the floor.

'Al,' she said to his father, 'what's the trouble this time?'

'Dust, Dot,' he replied.

'Don't "dust, Dot" me,' she said, 'I've got nothing to do with what goes on up here.' She turned to her son. 'Aren't you cold, Sam?'

'No, Mum.' Sam never noticed whether it was hot or cold in the attic; he had to concentrate too much on what he was doing. If he got things wrong there would be a terrible train crash.

'Controller!' His father's voice reached him from somewhere under the table.

'Yes, Dad.'

'Throw the switch!'

Sam bent over the control panel. He could work all the controls of the model railway, but this time it was very important to get everything right. Once, when he

was at the controls, he had made a mistake, there had
been a flash, and his father under the table had got a
nasty electric shock. Sam put his finger on a little lever
and pulled it back. 'I've thrown the switch!' he called.

This time there was no flash. But there was a big
shout. 'Blast it!' cried his father. It was a very large
table and his father was quite a distance away but his
voice seemed to make the whole attic shake. 'It didn't
work—there was no contact!'

'Why?' said Sam.

'Dust!' said Dad.

'I'm off,' said Dot, and her head began to disappear
through the floor.

'Hold on, Dot. Have you got that feather duster with
you?'

'I have, Al—but you're not going to have it up here
in this dirty old attic.'

'Just this once, Dot,' he pleaded. 'I'm in a very
awkward corner and I can't reach.'

'Oh, very well, but for the life of me I can't see
what you two find to keep you so busy up here—
there's not even a window.'

But Sam, from where he was sitting, was looking
over rooftops towards trees and the tower of a church.
And there was a postman cycling down to the bridge
where a boy and a girl were feeding ducks in a stream.
He knew them well—and the troublesome ducks who
were always sliding away on the glassy stream and
would never stay where you wanted them. He could
also see, in the distance, that there were people waiting
on the platform of a village railway station. They must
be getting impatient with what was going on under the
table.

'It's dark down here.' It was Dad's voice booming
away from somewhere out of sight. 'Be a good lad,

Sam, and fetch the duster from your mum—and a light.'

'OK, Dad.' He set all the controls at neutral and lowered himself from his stool. He went down quite slowly because he always enjoyed getting closer to the landscape with its ploughed fields of corduroy cut from an old pair of trousers, the streets and buses of the town, the tiny rabbits on the hillside above the railway tunnel, and the colours glowing through the stained glass he himself had installed in the church windows. But then, as he went further down, he was underground among the darkness and struts that held it all in place.

'You men and your train sets,' said Dot as Sam crawled towards her under the big layout that filled the attic. 'It looks to me as though you are going to need dusting just as much as all those bits and bobs you've got here.'

'Keeps us out of mischief,' he said, imitating her.

'Saucy young brute!' She whisked at him with the duster. 'Boys and their toys!' She clicked her tongue, tch tch. 'I don't know what you see in it.'

'Yes, you do,' he said.

They were both holding the feather duster and she tugged at it until she had pulled him closer until they were nose to nose. She smiled. 'Yes, I do like it,' she said. 'All those little houses and little people. It's marvellous what you and your dad have done. It looks real.'

'It *is* real.'

'That's what bothers me.' She was standing on the loft ladder with only her head and shoulders within the attic. 'The way you and Al talk, anyone would think the grass really grew on those fields, and those little people really moved.'

'They really look as if they do,' he said, 'when the trains are running.'

'When!' She was grinning and tugging him off balance. 'It takes all this gloomy cavern beneath the fields to keep them going. You and your father are just gnomes with dusters.'

The light from below caught the edges of her frizzy hair and made it glow. 'And you look like a dandelion,' he said and had to skitter into the gloom out of reach.

It was getting near Christmas, and Sam had been promised that next day they would go to the city to see the lights and visit Father Christmas in his grotto.

'It's cold,' said Dot. 'We've all got to wrap up.'

Sam knew what that meant, and tried to hide behind his father.

'Al,' said Dot, 'bring that boy to me at once.'

'You'd better do what your mother says, Sam. She's got that look on her face.'

And she also held a woolly hat with a bobble on top. 'You do not take one step out of this house unless this is on your head,' she said. 'It keeps you warm.'

'And I quite like it,' said Al.

'It's lovely,' said Dot.

'I hate it,' said Sam.

'Well,' said his father, 'it's a bit like a ticket, and they won't let you on the train without it.'

So Sam wore it and forgot about it as he watched the hedges and fences flicker past at the edge of the track as the frozen fields beyond them swung by more slowly and fell behind, and he forgot about it twice over when there was a fault somewhere along the line and they had to get off the train at a station they didn't want.

'Oh, what a disappointment!' said his mother, but then she spotted something. 'Look, there's the

Underground,' and there, on the next platform, was the entrance.

But when they got there it was only to find that the trains underground were not running either. 'It must be the signals,' said his father, 'but don't worry—we'll wait on the platform down below; it's warmer than up here.'

But it wasn't only the signals that had gone wrong; the escalator had also stopped and they had to go down a very long staircase. There were a lot of people and they all seemed to be in a hurry even though they were not going to miss their trains, because there weren't any trains to miss. They jostled by in both directions and soon there were several people between Sam and his mother and father, but he was able to keep them in view on the steep stairs so he wasn't worried.

At the bottom, however, it was different. He could see nothing but legs and feet, and whenever there was a gap in the swirl all he saw were the openings of tunnels leading to different platforms. He did not run because he did not know which way to go. He stood still and looked around very carefully—that was the best way to see his mother's frizzy hair or his father's hand holding the red travelling bag with their sandwiches, but every time he thought he caught a glimpse of them someone's coat flapped in front of his eyes and the next second they were gone.

Sam was beginning to feel frightened, but then he thought that his mother and father could not have gone very far because there were no trains running so, if he wandered to and fro very slowly in the same place, they would almost certainly see him before long. He let himself drift towards the edge of the crowd, always keeping his eyes on the tunnels. The lights were bright and they glinted so fiercely from the white tiles that

lined the walls that his eyes began to ache and he was glad when he found a quieter spot just to one side of the stairs where he was in shadow.

The air was different here, just as dusty but not quite so hot, and a draught pressed him gently in the back. He turned round and saw there was a space under the stairs quite tall enough for him to walk through and get to the other side. That would be useful for keeping a proper look-out, so he walked into the shadow. It was then that he discovered it was more than just a gap. There was a narrow doorway hidden in the wall under the stairs, and the door was open. He looked through into darkness, but the cool draught felt like the open air and he was sure he was looking into a huge empty space, a cavern hollowed out underground. And a sound floated towards him on the air. Something was rumbling in the distance, but it wasn't a train and it wasn't machinery; it sounded more like a deep voice, and it was saying something.

He took a step closer and leant inside the doorway. The sense of an enormous space stretching away into the distance was stronger than ever, and the deep grumble certainly had words in it. Somebody seemed to be saying, 'Send him home, send him home' over and over again. Send who? Sam peered into darkness and tested the ground. It was solid enough, so he took a step inside the cavern.

He looked back just once to make sure that the crowds at the foot of the stairs were within reach if he had to turn and run, and then took another pace. The voice became clearer but, as it did so, it seemed to be talking complete nonsense. 'Send me a gnome!' it moaned. 'Send me a gnome!'

Sam took another careful step, and then another, and he was about to advance further when a spark of

light in the distance startled him and he stopped. He looked around. He could just make out that he was in a huge tunnel with arched ribs curving high overhead. But there was no railway line in it, just a jumble of thick black wires and rods connected to bits of silent machinery. The only sound was the voice, and now it became suddenly much louder. It came rumbling and tumbling along the tunnel towards him like a great ball of sound and burst all around him. 'So there you are at last!' it roared. 'What took you so long?'

It could hardly be speaking to him for he could see nothing in the darkness, so Sam remained silent.

'Speak up!' said the voice, and when Sam still did not reply it boomed, 'Where's your tool box?'

'I haven't got one.' The words came out before Sam could stop them.

'What's the use of a gnome without a tool box! For the last half-hour I've been calling out "Send me a gnome! Send me a gnome!" . . . and then they send me one without a tool box!'

'But I'm not a gnome,' said Sam.

There was a deep silence and the light in the distance was blotted out as something of great size moved there. Sam could hear a shuffling like big cushiony footsteps, and breathing huge enough to send tiles rattling from rooftops, but as there were no rooftops it whistled in the tunnel like a gale. Then the footsteps stopped and the voice came again. 'You look like a gnome to me,' it said. 'I suppose you'll be telling me next you know nothing about railways.'

Sam wondered if he should answer, but then risked saying in a small voice, 'I've got a railway at home.'

'So have I . . . ' the voice came down like an avalanche ' . . . and this is it!'

'You mean all the trains down here?' Sam asked.

'And up top! All those trains up there among the fields and houses. I've got to keep 'em all running . . . and then something has to go wrong with the switches under the tracks and they all stop. Do you know what I mean, gnome?'

Sam was about to answer when a light came on and he saw who was speaking to him. The light was a torch held in a man's hand—a big man, so big he had to stoop to avoid banging his head against the tunnel's high roof, but now he crouched down to take a better look at the boy in front of him. It was a huge face, so large that it would never have got through a barn door, and a lot of breathing came through its nostrils, but there was nothing angry about it even though its eyebrows went up at the sight of Sam and came down in a frown as it squinted to take a closer look. The giant's nose twitched.

'I think I'm going to sneeze,' he said. 'You'd better hang on to something.'

Sam only had time to grip one of the tunnel's steel ribs before the giant turned his head away and a great bellow of a sneeze thundered around them and went echoing away into the distance while Sam hung on to prevent himself going with it.

'Dust!' roared the giant in a voice almost as terrible as the sneeze. 'That's what does it. Dust!' His eyes, still watering from the sneeze, were turned on Sam. 'Did I hear you say something?' he asked.

Sam shook his head.

'Gnomes generally say something about the dust,' said the giant. 'And about what a problem it is for me, working here all alone.'

'Well . . . ' Sam began, then didn't know how to go on.

'Well . . . ?' The giant raised his eyebrows and waited for an answer.

'The only thing I know about dust,' said Sam uncertainly, 'is that it causes a lot of trouble with my trains. It gets to the bits hidden away underneath the tracks and jams the switches just in the places you can't reach.'

'Snap!' roared the giant. 'That's exactly what's happened down here. The dust has got into the main treble-toggle three-way master switch and has cut out the entire system and stopped all the trains—and I can't reach it because I'm too big!'

'I know what you mean,' said Sam.

'You know? How do you know?'

'Because it happens to us. Things go wrong under the layout and my dad's too big to get at it properly . . . even though he's not quite as big as you.'

'That's exactly why I sent for a gnome,' said the giant. 'What does your dad do?'

'He sends for me.'

'Ah!' The giant's eyes widened. 'So you *are* a gnome—your dad's gnome.'

'Sort of,' said Sam.

The giant's huge eyes looked Sam up and down very carefully. 'Do you suppose . . . ' he rumbled, then paused to think it over. 'No, I don't think so. You are a bit bigger than the normal type of gnome and my problem is in a very awkward place . . . it would be far too tight a spot, even for you.'

'I wouldn't mind trying.'

'You'd get stuck,' said the giant. 'Nothing's more certain.' But his eyes still rested on Sam, and after keeping silent for a long moment he cleared his throat and said, 'However, that is a very fine hat you have on your head.'

And Sam realized he was still wearing the hat with the ridiculous bobble.

'I like the woolly bit on top,' said the giant. 'It might just do the trick.'

'What trick?'

The giant put out his hand and lifted his little finger. 'Do you think your hat might fit this?'

'We can try,' said Sam, and he took the hat off his head and put it over the tip of the giant's finger.

'A perfect fit!' The giant was delighted. 'I think we have made an important discovery.' His smile was wider than Sam could have measured with both arms.

Together they went down the tunnel to where there was a great clump of wires and a complicated piece of machinery in the roof. 'There's where the trouble is,' said the giant. 'The dust is clogging up the switch just behind there.' He reached up to a small gap in the roof, put out his little finger with the bobble hat on its tip and poked it into the gap. 'That little furry bit on top is just the thing for dust.' He wriggled his finger. 'Nearly there . . . nearly there . . . Ah!'

There was a sizzle, a bang, and a flash. 'Done it!' he roared, and lights sprang up all along the tunnel. 'Listen!'

Sam heard nothing, but then, through the soles of his shoes, he felt a tremble in the ground and then a rumble came from overhead.

'Young gnome!' cried the giant, 'the trains are running—and all thanks to you!'

He took the woolly hat from his finger and put it back on Sam's head, and they walked back along the tunnel to the doorway.

'Thank you for your help,' said the giant, 'but I hope you won't tell anyone what has just happened. It's a bit embarrassing if people find out that I need gnomes to help me—and if the news gets around I might lose my job.'

'I promise,' said Sam, and a moment later found himself at the foot of the staircase. People were still rushing by, but now there was also the rumble of trains.

'So there you are,' said his father. 'I told your mum you'd have the sense to stand still and wait for us to find you.'

But his mother was looking at his hat. 'What on earth have you done to your bobble?' she cried. 'It's smouldering!'

Sam just grinned, and stood there like a chimney with a wisp of smoke rising above his head.

Train Boy to the Rescue

NICOLA ROBINSON

Train Boy was a small green plastic figure, which had come in a Christmas cracker. I thought it looked like a seasick elf, but Aiden saw it differently. 'He's a superhero from Planet Ergon in the fifty-second galaxy,' he told me. 'Tougher than tough. Stronger than strong.' Train Boy's daily mission was to save Aiden's toy trains from tumbling over cliffs, derailing into fields of dynamite, invasions by monsters from outer space, all kinds of dire disaster.

Aiden also said that every rescue was for real; that somewhere in the great big world beyond Berry, Australia, a train was able to keep on chugging because of Train Boy's incredible feats. My little brother was a spooky kid—he could sometimes tell who was on the phone the moment it started ringing, funny things like that—but I wasn't buying his Train Boy story. Well you wouldn't, would you?

Aiden's train set was his favourite thing, crummy as it was. He used to stare boggle-eyed at pictures of those old-fashioned electric train sets, with perfect replicas of

famous trains chuffing over plaster-of-paris bridges and painted rivers and what-have-you, but my parents didn't have that sort of money, so Aiden didn't have that sort of train set. His was plastic, with lots of short black lengths of line that slotted together like a jigsaw, and a bunch of no-frills choo-choo trains in yellow, red, and silver. But to listen to the stories he came out with (and we had no choice about that, because he shouted them at the top of his voice) you'd think every great train in history was racing round our lounge room.

The evening of my eleventh birthday was no different. Aiden announced that the Burlington Zephyr was hauling through a terrifyingly steep and rocky canyon—that is, between two cushions on the lounge room floor. 'Woooo-wooo!' he shrieked.

'Shut up, Aiden!' I yelled over my shoulder.

'Sshhhhhhh!' Mum called from the kitchen.

'Emergency! Emergency! Landslide! Line blocked! Train Boy to the rescue!'

'Aiden, SHUT UP!' I shouted. This time I must have sounded like I meant it, because he stopped yelling. All I could hear was the whirr of toy train wheels in the lounge room. Then silence. No crashes or smashes, so Train Boy must have done it again: averted disaster at the last nano-second.

Then, 'Woooo-wooo!' Aiden began again.

This time I ignored him. I was standing at my bedroom window, waiting for the southbound 7.01 to poke its nose out from between the hills, a couple of kilometres down the line. Dad was on that train, and I wanted him home so I could have my birthday dinner and cake—and the new bike he was bringing down from Sydney. My first bike.

We live right on the South Coast commuter line, so

close that if you walk to the end of our section (stamping loudly to scare off the black snakes), then poke your arm through the wire fence, you can feel the breeze from the trains as they whizz past. Not that we're allowed to do this, and not that I've been bothered for a long time. They're not exactly world class trains, just old red rattlers and new silver rattlers, better at being slow and late than anything else.

That was the problem tonight. Dad's train was late, ten minutes late already. 'Come on, come on, come on,' I whispered, pressing my face against the glass, which was still warm from the hot February day.

I willed the train to round that corner, slip behind the cluster of gum trees, pass the other two old farmhouses in our valley—the first weatherbeaten cream, the second faded blue—race past our house, then all the way to Berry station.

But it didn't.

'The Silver Streak is pulling away from the station! Choo-choo-choo-choo, choo-choo-choo-choo!' yelled Aiden.

'Put a sock in it, trainbrain,' I said, wandering into the lounge room.

'Sshhh!' Mum called from the kitchen.

'You know, Hannah,' said Aiden, who was sitting in the middle of the floor, surrounded by plastic train tracks, 'when you blow out the candles and make your birthday wish, you could wish to be a less bossy person.'

'Gee, Aiden,' I said. 'What a nice idea. Or maybe I could wish for a seven-year-old brother whose voice matched his brain size: very small.' I marched into Dad's study, on the other side of the house from my room. I guess it was dumb, but I was trying to trick Dad's train. If I stopped watching, it would have to come.

Aiden started up again, 'The Silver Streak is pushing onwards, through the . . . '

I couldn't help myself. I peeked out of the window, because it was just possible that Dad's train had passed in the thirty seconds I'd spent walking from bedroom to study, and I would see it on this side of the house, heading up to the station.

'The Silver Streak is taking the corner, into the bush . . .'

'Sshhh!' Mum called from the kitchen.

Dad's train wasn't there, but it was nice to look out of his window anyway. There's a thick patch of bush on this side of our house, and the peeling trunks of the gum trees were a dozen shades of brown and gold in the evening sun. It was so dazzling that I could have missed it: a flicker of silver between the trees, coming from the south. Where it shouldn't have been.

'Danger! Danger! Early warning activated!'

'Shut up!' I yelled. My belly was flip-flopping. There's only a single line of track between the Berry station and our house. That silver train was on it and Dad's train was due to be on it too, coming from the opposite direction.

'Danger! Woooo-ooo, woooo-ooo, woooo-ooo!'

I turned and raced back to my bedroom, leaping over Aiden's train set.

'Hey!' he yelled, though I hadn't touched so much as a plastic caboose.

'Sshhh!' Mum called from the kitchen.

Standing at my window, I bit my lip. 'Please don't come, train,' I whispered. 'Be late, be late, be very, very late.' For a few seconds nothing happened. I drew a long breath. It had all been my imagination. Then—

'Two engines on the line! Collision imminent!'

In the distance, Dad's train appeared. It was a tired

old red rattler. No wonder it was late. For a moment I thought about my birthday. My bike.

'Warning! Warning!'

I raced out of my room and tripped over Aiden, falling flat on my face.

'Hey!' he yelled again. 'Get off!' I didn't bother to answer. As I picked myself up I saw that he had now made two hills from the cushions, and run his train tracks over them. A train was sliding snail-like down each hill—the train set is so useless that the engines have no speed at all unless pushed. But slow or not these trains, one red and one silver, were headed for a collision.

I stumbled to Dad's room. The silver train was closer. I could make out its dark glass stripe of window, worming in the distance beyond the bush. I ran to my own room. The red rattler was picking up speed in the flat valley, about to slip behind the cluster of gum trees.

'The Red Demon is on the way! Danger! Danger!'

'Sshhh!' Mum called from the kitchen. I was too scared to say anything at all.

I dashed to the study. The silver train was glowing ominously. It would reach our section in about a minute. Back again. The red rattler was close, too close, just passing the old cream farmhouse, less than a minute away. I didn't have time to phone the station. I didn't have time to run down to the train line, waving a red flag. I didn't have time to think.

Who could help?

'Train Boy to the rescue!' shouted Aiden. 'Zooming in from Planet Ergon! Can he make it? Can he do it?'

I whirled around and into the lounge room. Aiden was standing by the fireplace, Train Boy held high, poised to fly down between the plastic trains, which by now were only centimetres apart.

Suddenly I heard a terrible, wrenching screech. I ran to Dad's window. The silver train was braking, but it was only about fifty metres away.

'Uh-oh! Train Boy attacked by cosmic grizzly!' yelled Aiden. As I ran back through the lounge room I saw Train Boy tussling with a tiny teddy bear, as Aiden knelt beside the toy trains—close enough to stop them, if the stupid bear would let Train Boy do it.

Then the screech of brakes became twice as loud. From my bedroom I could see the red train, only seconds away. It was braking too.

The silver train came into view on my right. The red train was still racing forward, too fast, on my left. There was only one person to turn to, and suddenly, despite being eleven years old, despite knowing better, despite everything—I was ready to do it.

I leapt into the lounge room, just in time to see Aiden punch the teddy bear so hard that it sailed through the air and thumped into the bookshelf.

'Go, Train Boy! Go, Train Boy!' I screamed, clenching my fists.

'Sshhh!' Mum called from the kitchen.

Train Boy flew to the track, stood on the rails, and stopped one train with each hand. I whirled around to face my window, so scared that I couldn't breathe. The two steaming, juddering trains come to a halt. The distance between them was the span of a young boy's arms.

I turned slowly back to Aiden, who was looking up at me with a strange little smile. 'I guess Dad will be home soon,' he said softly. 'You'll get your bike. Happy Birthday, Hannah.'

I took a shaky breath. I had been begging for that bike for months, but right then I wouldn't have cared if a dastardly destroyer from Planet X had dumped it at

the bottom of the sea. I sat down beside my little brother, wrapped my arms around him, and kissed him all over his face.

'Eee-yuck!' said Aiden, but he nuzzled his head against my shoulder, just for a moment or two. Then he swung around to a different section of plastic track, grabbed a yellow train and shouted, 'The Union Pacific is on the line, westward bound!' And I didn't mind a bit.

Cabbage Soup

ALISON PRINCE

George stood with his parents, Mike and Elvira, waiting
for a bus in Euston Road. He read out what it said on
the ones that went past. 'Putney, Hammersmith, Stoke
Newington.' Then he added, 'Ours won't be one of
these red ones, will it?'

'No,' said Mike. 'Double deckers don't go to
Hungary.'

'Why aren't we going by train?' asked George. 'I
mean, it's going to be a train to China, isn't it?'

'Cheaper by bus to Budapest,' said a man called Les in
a strong Yorkshire accent. 'I'll buy Trans-Siberian tickets
there, see. Pay for 'em in forints.' He wore a donkey
jacket with shiny waterproof shoulders and carried no
luggage except a small Army rucksack and a clipboard.

A woman in a tweed hat glanced at her watch and
said, 'We're already four minutes late. I do hope these
people know what they're doing.'

'Artisan Tours has run more trips than you've had
hot dinners,' said Les. 'So we'll have no alarm and
despondency, thank you very much.'

The tweed-hat woman turned to her tweed-hatted husband and said, 'Trevor, I think we may have made a mistake.'

Trevor prodded with his shooting-stick at a cigarette-end on the pavement and said, 'They're all as bad. Remember Bangkok?'

Then a bus came that had a bit of cardboard in the window saying BUDAPEST, so they all got in.

The afternoon grew darker as they drove across France, and Charlie the driver leaned forward to fiddle with the switches. Then he stopped the bus and opened and shut the door several times.

'Trouble?' asked Les.

'Lights won't go on,' said Charlie. 'Not unless door's open.' He came from Yorkshire as well.

'So we drive wi' door open,' said Les. 'Bit cold, but it won't kill 'em.'

Charlie shook his head. 'Bus won't go wi' door open,' he said. 'Electrical cut-out. Safety.'

'Can you fix it?' asked Les.

'No,' said Charlie. 'Have to phone.'

So Les ordered a brew-up. He and some of the old hands who had travelled with Artisan Tours before opened the side of the bus and got out a gas stove and a huge black kettle which took a very long time to boil.

'All got your mugs?' Les bellowed when the tea was at last made and a man in overalls was fixing the lights. 'You were told to bring mugs.'

Trevor and Mavis had disappeared.

'Two missing,' Les said when he counted everyone back into the mended bus. 'Who is it?'

'Tweed hats,' said one of the girls who sat on the back seat with her friends, and they all giggled.

'Would be, wouldn't it,' said Les.

Everyone sat in nervous silence until Charlie said, 'Here they come.' He flashed the lights and hooted the horn, but Trevor and Mavis didn't hurry. When they climbed aboard, Mavis said, 'We found a very decent little café.'

'Did you,' Les said grimly. 'Well, I hope you find one in Budapest and all, because we're going to miss the train to Moscow.'

He was right. And the next one wasn't until midnight.

The station buffet was a large, rather grand room that smelt of something hot and spicy. 'I'm starving,' said George.

They settled down to bowls of goulash soup and hunks of bread, and people started getting to know each other. The girls who sat on the back seat were being chatted up by two Irish plumbers called Eamonn and Patrick, and Trevor and Mavis were playing bridge with a grey-haired couple from Edinburgh. Elvira got her sketch-book out, and Mike was talking railways with a fellow-enthusiast. 'Absolutely got to see these steam locos while the Chinese are still using them,' George heard him say.

Eamonn started playing a tune on a tin whistle, and Mavis glanced across and frowned.

'Have you got a headache?' a woman in a patchwork jacket asked her. 'I could give you some Tiger Balm.'

'No, thank you,' said Mavis.

'Or massage,' the woman went on. 'I'm good at massage.'

'You can massage me any time you like,' said Patrick. 'What's your name?'

'Mercy Grainger,' said the woman, and Eamonn broke

into a tune George recognized as 'Country Gardens', because they had a tape of it at school, for when they went out of Assembly. But he laughed, getting the joke, and said, 'That's by *Percy* Grainger, not Mercy.'

'Now there's a boy for you,' said Patrick. 'All the knowledge in the world, and him not a day more than twelve.'

'Ten, actually,' said George.

The bridge players were shuffling their cards and telling each other about previous trips they'd been on, all of which sounded disastrous.

' . . . Sorrento. Couldn't swing a cat.'

' . . . realized we'd left it in the taxi. Never got it back, of course.'

Everyone was listening for what would come next, though they were pretending not to. Eamonn stopped playing, and Mavis's voice was loud in the silence. 'You'd think they'd make a decent curry in Bombay. "My dear man," I said, "you need sultanas".'

Patrick choked with laughter on his Hungarian beer and had to be slapped on the back by Eamonn and anyone who fancied joining in. Trevor looked across, and George heard him say, 'This is what you get, of course, when you do things on the cheap.'

The toilets on the train to Budapest were unbelieveably smelly and the sheets on the narrow bunks felt slightly damp, but George didn't care. After the previous night of trying to sleep on the bus as it rolled through Germany and Austria, just lying flat was great.

Early the next morning, George woke to the sound of heavy clanging. He looked out of the compartment

window to find that the train was in a huge shed, and his coach was suspended in the air between two vast, yellow-painted jacks.

'Changing the wheels,' Mike said happily. 'We're at the Russian border, and their railways are a wider gauge.'

'Absurd,' Mavis was saying in the corridor. 'All this delay. Why did the Russians have to be different?'

Mike went out to explain. 'They're the ones who *aren't* different. We all used the five-foot gauge at first, then we put the flange on the wheels instead of the rails, reducing the width to four feet, eight and a half inches. Do you see?'

'No,' said Mavis. She glanced at George and added, 'I expect your little boy is getting rather bored. This is hardly the trip for a child, is it?'

George was outraged. 'I'm not bored!' he said. 'It's much better than India. And Peru—'

Mavis went into her compartment and shut the door.

After a couple of days in Moscow, they assembled at Jaroslavski Station on Friday evening to board the Trans-Siberian Express, along with hundreds of other people. Women with shawls over their heads sat among large bundles and boxes tied with string, and emotional goodbyes were being said. There was no sign of the train. George looked up at the big clock and saw the minute hand tick along to nine o'clock—and the train was due to leave at ten past.

'Never known to be late,' said Mike. 'You'll see.' George thought his father was being a bit rash, but sure enough, the train slid slowly in to the platform, dark green and immensely long, with three steps up to

its high doors, same as the one from Budapest. There was frantic shoving of baggage and people to get all the stuff aboard amid hugging and kissing and making the sign of the cross, and then the train was moving, dead on ten past nine as Mike had said, beginning its six-day journey to China. In every compartment, people were climbing up to stow luggage in the space above the corridor and stuffing things under the bottom bunk. George and his parents were in with Mercy Grainger and two elderly ladies called Nancy and Dot.

A dark-haired man in a black-and-brown patterned shirt appeared at the door and said, '*Ya provodnik*. Sasha.'

'Oh, good,' said Nancy. '*Preevyet*, Sasha.' She shook hands with the man and explained, 'He's our coach attendant.'

'*Ya* Dot,' said Dot.

'Dot?' Sasha seemed puzzled.

'Dot, *da*,' said Dot. 'Short for Dorothy.'

'*Ya* George,' said George, getting the idea.

Sasha smiled and ruffled George's hair. '*Chai hochesh?*' he enquired, and waved an arm to indicate the end of the corridor. 'Samovar. OK?'

'OK,' said George.

'We can have tea when we want it,' Nancy explained when Sasha had gone. 'From the samovar.'

George went to look, hoping the samovar would be a mad thing that looked a bit like the World Cup, but it was just a hot-water boiler that fed the radiators in the coach, with glasses for tea stacked on top of it round a small, black teapot. Sasha turned up and poured a little very strong tea from the pot into a glass in a metal holder, topped it up with hot water from the samovar's tap and gave it to George. '*Spasseeba*,' he said helpfully.

'*Spasseeba*,' George repeated, and hoped it was the Russian for Thank You.

The next morning, it was snowing. Big, fluffy flakes fell from a dark sky, and the ground between the fir trees outside was white. Inside the train, the corridors and compartments were warm, but George found that the floor of the tiny toilet was covered with ice. Sasha appeared with a bucket of hot water and sloshed it about, poking with an iron bar at the frozen-over hole in the middle of the floor until the melted ice ran through. Then he threw down a bit of old blanket for a foothold when the floor froze again, and went off to brush with a birch-twig broom at the snow that had drifted in where the coaches joined.

The joining-places were quite exciting, George thought. The overlapping metal plates were slippery with ice, and on either side of them you could see down to the track rushing underneath. There was a thin grab-rail inside the black concertina walls, but it was so cold that your hand stuck to it if you weren't wearing gloves.

Trevor and Mavis said they couldn't possibly walk over the joining-places, they were much too dangerous—but there wasn't any choice. The dining car was at the end of the train, seven coaches away, and you got there or went without.

'I'm going to put on pounds,' Elvira said after a couple of days. 'Pork chops for breakfast, and all this black bread and mashed potatoes and cabbage soup. Pass the salt, please.'

Mavis shuddered. 'The cabbage soup is *dreadful*,' she said. 'There's always a lump of gristly meat in the bottom.'

'Not if you're a vegetarian,' Mercy Grainger said a little smugly. 'You get a slice of lemon instead. I'm running yoga sessions in the corridor, if you feel a bit over-stuffed.'

Mike was still full of enthusiasm. 'Brilliant, isn't it,' he said, 'the way they have coal for the samovars waiting on the platforms, and food supplies. All in the middle of nowhere.'

'They keep the bread under the seats,' said George. 'One of the girls had to get up yesterday because the waiter wanted another loaf.'

'Quite the little know-all, aren't we,' said Mavis.

George opened his mouth to say something, but Mike gave him a nudge and made a funny face. So he got on with his cabbage soup.

Meal-times, according to people's watches, became a bit odd as the train went further east. All Russian railways ran on Moscow time, so by Tuesday, breakfast was at half past four in the morning.

'I'm confused,' said Patrick, holding his head.

'You always have been,' said Eamonn.

Mercy Grainger smiled peacefully and told them to go by the sun and the moon, and George wondered what the fuss was about. He didn't have a watch, so he was quite happy.

The day before they were due to reach the Chinese border, Sasha went into a frenzy of vacuuming the corridors and changing sheets, and the dining car served a special breakfast of caviar, meat-balls, and—wonder of wonders—chips. 'It's like they want to prove they do things better than the Chinese,' said Dot. 'Sweet, really.'

Then Sasha found that one of the tea-glasses was missing, complete with its metal holder, and told Nancy in utter gloom that he would have to pay for it. Four roubles. Les organized a whip-round. 'And if I find out some miserable so-and-so pinched it for a souvenir, I'll have his guts for garters,' he said.

Trevor and Mavis refused to contribute to the tea-glass fund, and so did a couple called Ron and Audrey who kept a pub in Streatham. 'The chap probably does it every time,' said Ron. 'Nice way to get a fat tip out of the tourists.' Les gave him a dirty look and went off to see Sasha, who was so pleased to get the money that he produced a bottle of cherry brandy. It led to an impromptu party that went on all the way to Manchuria.

After a long wait for wheel-changing and inspections by Russian officials then Chinese ones, the train got going again. Everyone trooped along for supper at the very normal time of half past six, because Moscow time had been left behind at the frontier, along with the Russian dining car.

'I say!' said Trevor, staring round. 'That's more like it!'

The Chinese dining car had tasselled red silk lanterns all down the middle, and the tables were laid with white cloths and chopsticks.

'No more cabbage soup!' said Mavis.

George didn't say anything. He rather missed the gloomy-looking Russian waiter who sometimes got excited about a football team called Dynamo—and the cabbage soup had been all right. He wasn't sure about the Chinese food. Some of it looked like chopped-up rubber bands.

Mike was too happy to care. At the border, he'd managed to get on the foot-plate of the steam locomotive

that was now pulling the train, and he still had a smudge of black grease on his nose. Elvira said she reckoned he'd never wash it off.

George wasn't really into steam engines, even though he'd been called after George Stephenson, who invented the Rocket. When he went to bed in his narrow bunk that night, he could feel it jiggling as if the whole train was vibrating to the piston-beats of the loco. It felt a bit funny, but he didn't complain.

Mavis did, of course. She said she hadn't slept a wink. Mercy said she could have had a Golden Slumbers tea-bag, but Mavis just shuddered. George began to wish something truly dreadful would happen to her and Trevor.

Before dawn the next morning, the train was moving past small houses and hard-pruned trees on the outskirts of Beijing.

'Look!' said Mercy in excitement. 'People doing t'ai chi!'

George stared out at the little figures moving very slowly in the grey light, and thought it was weird—and so was their arrival time at the terminus station. Why six thirty-one?

'Never a minute late,' said Mike proudly.

There was no snow here, and after the Siberian winter they had come through, the dry, cool air seemed almost warm. The Chinese took them to a big hotel for a rather nasty breakfast of gluey dumplings in chicken soup, then they were dumped by bus at a museum, though everyone was longing for a shower and a bed you could sit up in without hitting your head.

In the days that followed, they were taken to temples, gift-shops, schools, a Typical Worker's Flat, a crane factory, more gift-shops, the Great Wall of China, more temples, and an underground network of

tunnels, complete with hospital and concert-hall, in case Beijing should be invaded. The train enthusiasts went to the engine works at Harbin, and the others to another temple.

After the crane factory, Mavis had a headache every morning, and she and Trevor spent their time in the Hotel Beijing, where they served English tea and crumpets.

It was a different *provodnik* on the way back. Nicolai, a fair-haired giant, was so good-looking that the girls were in a constant state of the flutters, and the dining car was presided over (once they were out of China) by a solid lady with her hair screwed up into a bun and a waitress in a brown skirt who wore grey socks over her tights. The first Russian breakfast was at two-thirty a.m. by Moscow time, and lunch was at seven in the morning. Mavis was in full grumbling mode.

'Cabbage soup again. Honestly, Trevor, I can't put up with this much longer.'

'We'll pop out at stations,' said Trevor. 'See what we can buy.'

People had always got out when the train made a fifteen-minute stop, to stretch the legs and breathe the ferociously icy air, but Trevor and Mavis were now in search of a station kiosk. They came back with vanilla-flavoured buns and greasy turnovers wrapped in squares of paper. They weren't the only ones, but they were always first out and last back.

At Krasnojarsk, Patrick went out without his jacket for a dare, and caught a chill that had him shivering under his blanket with a high temperature. Nicolai came and looked at him, then went off to his cubbyhole by the samovar to radio for a doctor, who came aboard at the next stop. He took Patrick's temperature and pointed to an English-Russian phrase-book. YOU MUST GO TO HOSPITAL.

'Can't do that,' said Les. 'Visas run out in four days.'

The doctor shrugged and handed out some large pink pills which had Patrick on his feet again that evening, and got off at the next station.

The Trans-Siberian was a little world of its own, George thought. The fir trees and the snow went past outside as if the windows were just TV screens and everything real was in here. Nicolai had the radio on a lot, playing soulful Russian music, though it caused more complaints from the bridge-playing compartment, and Mercy was making yogurt on the radiator and Dot was telling fortunes—there was plenty going on. No need to be bored.

And then it happened.

The train stopped at Omsk in the middle of the night and George, warm and sleepy in his bunk, looked out past the edge of the blind to where a few people stood round a dimly-lit kiosk. The station clock said 1.45. Coal was being hauled aboard, and crates of milk and the stuff called *kefir* in green bottles. And bread, and cabbages. A man in a long coat and a fur hat got on, carrying a black bag, and George wondered idly if someone else had been taken ill, because he looked like a doctor.

The train began to slide quietly out of the station. Two people turned from the kiosk, with their arms waving like excited puppets. They started to run across the platform, their mouths open as if they were shouting. And George saw that they were Trevor and Mavis.

He stared as if hypnotized, and waited for a commotion to start in their compartment next door

when Ron and Audrey realized they'd gone. None
came, and the train gathered speed.

'I didn't see them until it was too late,' he said the next
morning, feeling a bit guilty.

'Not your fault, lad,' said Les. 'The Russkis'll sort
'em out. Nicolai's been on the blower to Omsk.'

'But they're all alone in the middle of Siberia, with
no luggage!' said Elvira. 'And their visas are going to
run out, and they don't speak Russian!'

There was a short silence, then Les said, 'That'll
give 'em summat to grumble about.'

Suddenly everyone was falling about with laughter,
because it was so awful, you couldn't do anything else.
Nicolai appeared, beaming, to say that a woman five
coaches along had given birth to a baby girl at three
o'clock this morning, and Eamonn said, 'It's time we
had a party. To celebrate.'

And so they did. They partied all the way to
Moscow, pausing only for mealtimes. And nobody
complained about the cabbage soup.

The Circle Game

LINDA NEWBERY

I first notice him, this kid, when a whole wodge of people gets out at Cannon Street. Till now it's been strap-hanging, extra passengers shoving themselves in at the door, everyone scanning the adverts or reading their papers. I've been here long enough to get a seat, so I've got a close-up view of some bloke's hairy wrist and smart watch, and a woman's shoulder bag hanging about three inches from my nose. I can smell the leather—black, expensive, and it's fastened with one of those press-stud clasps. Tempting—she's got her nose in a book and her mouth slightly open, engrossed. I bet there's a wallet in that bag, or a purse, stuffed with notes and credit cards.

But not all that tempting.

Then everyone sways and lurches as the train stops. The doors hiss open, and the people left standing take the empty seats. Most of them'll get out at Embankment.

I don't know how long this kid's been there, but he's clocked me before I notice him. He stands out, in the middle of all those office people. I suppose I must do,

too, cos this boy's looking at me like I'm the only person
he recognizes in that silent carriage. He's never seen me
before but he can tell we belong to the same club.

I don't mean the sort of club you pay to belong to. I
don't mean the sort with strobe lights and thumping
music, either. I mean, I can tell straight away he's done
a runner: all the signs are there. He's wearing a black
anorak that's too big for him, and the pockets are
stuffed full. He's holding a rucksack on his knees, and
he's got one arm round it like he thinks someone might
snatch it. His eyes and nose look a bit snively. Biggest
giveaway of all, he doesn't know where he's going.

His eyes keep flicking up to the strip of tube map
above the seats. Those names—South Kensington,
Edgware Road, Blackfriars—it's my map of the world,
but to him it might as well be the Planet Zarg. He's
going to London. That's where everyone goes. Well,
this is it, mate—London. What you going to do now?

He's around my age—about twelve. A scrawny kid,
with straggly hair that flops over his face. Not much of
a survivor. He'll give up—turn round and go back to
his nice cosy warm house. I look at his tight, anxious
face and start to guess. Trouble, yeah? You've been
grounded and you don't think it's fair? You don't get
on with your step-dad? You want to show them they
can't boss you around?

Been there. Seen it. Done it.

People are folding up their newspapers and moving
to the doors as the train slows for Embankment. The
doors sigh open, passengers spill out, two more get on.
While the train stands silent, I see Runner hesitate—he
clutches his rucksack more tightly and half stands up,
then realizes he's too late. He sits down with a defeated
look. He glances at me, sees me looking, and pretends
to be reading the adverts.

I decide to introduce him to the Circle Game. See if he'll follow.

I don't look at him again. The train moves on; the tunnel wall blurs into blackness. I sit looking at my own reflection. When the train stops at Victoria, I stand up suddenly, and get out. A glance back shows me Runner still sitting there, watching me—then, just as the doors are closing, he gets up and shoves his way out, pushing past a woman in a smart black coat, who tuts and glares.

Gotcha!

I know he'll stick with me now.

I don't look back again. I walk quickly, dodging commuters, weaving round dawdlers. Down stairs, round a curve of corridor, ride the escalator down to Victoria Line Northbound. Then, without a pause, I double back up the escalator, up the stairs, back to Circle Line Eastbound. And now I hardly dare check he's behind me—what if he isn't? Loneliness is a black hollow in my chest. But when I get to the platform, I do a quick look out of the corner of my eye. He's there—following me like my shadow's detached itself. I stop walking, he stops walking—a good way back, far enough to pretend he's got there by coincidence. But when the next train sweeps in, pushing a blast of hot tunnel air in front of it, he scurries along so's he can get in the same carriage.

I laugh silently. The bloke sitting opposite lowers his *Times* and I think he's heard me, but he's only brushing a bit of fluff off his trousers. I can do what I like now. At Westminster, I get out, dodge through to Circle Line Westbound, and get on a Paddington train. Runner's still there, my obedient little follower, loyal as

a sheepdog. I've become his only certainty in the huge, uncertain city.

I can get used to this. I like it, to tell you straight. It gives me a feeling of power. Besides that, I like the company—even if it's only the company of a snivelling little kid whose chances of surviving in the city are less than a pigeon's. I start to think about the home he's run away from. Nice room of his own, I bet. Computer. Meal on the table every evening. Kettle in the kitchen, biscuits in the cupboard—hot drinks whenever he wants them.

I shiver.

A bed and a duvet. Soft pillows. The comforting darkness of a sleeping house.

If he doesn't want all that, if that bed's empty, and the computer unused, maybe I could—

Don't be daft. I'm playing the Circle Game. This time, I stay in my seat, doing nothing, listening to the recorded voice call out the names. I could recite them in my sleep. Paddington, Edgware Road, Baker Street, Great Portland, Warren Street, Euston Square. It's changeover time now. All the office workers are at their desks now, for eight hours of whatever they do, till they come piling out at five o'clock and clog up the Underground again. It's the shoppers' shift now. People out for the day, often in pairs. Commuters hardly ever talk—it's a kind of rule—but shoppers do. They talk about where they'll have lunch, or why they're taking this pair of shoes back. Later, heading home before the office rush, they'll pile on the trains and clutter up the alleyways with carrier bags. There are a couple of students with Walkmans. There are mums with little kids who whine and moan and fidget.

There's one opposite me now, where the *Times* man was sitting till he got out at Paddington. A little fair-

haired kid, about three or four, in a quilted coat and brand-new Kickers. She knows what they're for. *Kick, kick,* she's going, against the seat. She whinges at her mum, who's trying to read a magazine. Mum's hand delves into a shopping bag and comes out with a bar of chocolate. The kid's happy now. She peels back the paper. She's looking at me as if to say *I bet you wish you had some* and then she breaks off two squares of chocolate and eats them with her mouth open.

I stare back and then, abruptly, pull my most ferocious face, the one that scares even me when I see it reflected in the window. The kid whimpers and snuggles up against her mum, who's too busy with *Home and Garden* to notice.

Serves you right, I think, you pampered little bundle of me-me-me. She keeps darting scared little glances my way, still eating chocolate and getting it all round her mouth, till her mum notices we're at Barbican and hauls her off.

Chocolate. I can imagine it, filling my mouth, bulging my cheeks. The hard corners dissolving to creaminess, the rich slow slide of it down my throat. If there's a machine on one of the platforms, I'll get some later— I've got a few coins, coins that have slid out of people's pockets and got wedged down the sides of the seats. I glance towards the far end of the carriage. Runner's eating too now, cramming crisps into his mouth. The carriage has emptied. At Liverpool Street the two remaining passengers get out and we're on our own.

He starts to move towards me, not looking, pretending to gaze up at the line map, standing by the door. He's not going to desert me, is he? But when the train stops at Aldgate, he doesn't press the button. The doors stay shut. He comes my way, holding out a packet of chewing-gum.

'Want some?'

I nod and take it. He sits next to me and dumps his rucksack. I can see the salty greasiness of crisps round his mouth, a few flaky bits sticking to the front of his anorak.

'Where you getting off?' he asks.

I shrug. 'South Ken. Notting Hill Gate. Doesn't make much difference.'

'Where you going, then?'

'Nowhere. Circle Line, that's where I'm going.' I slide the strip of gum into my mouth. Its spearmint taste is a cheat. It lasts only minutes, then you're just chewing and chewing on something tasteless that only makes you more hungry.

He stares at me. 'Round and round, yeah? You . . . go round and round on the Circle Line?'

I nod.

'How long you been doing that, then?'

'About—fifteen years,' I say.

He leans back, incredulous. 'You're winding me up! How old are you, then?'

'Twelve,' I say.

'You're twelve, but—' He opens his mouth in a soundless, disbelieving laugh. 'How d'you make that out, then?'

I shrug. Believe it or don't believe it. No odds to me.

'Why don't you get off? Aren't you fed up with it?'

I don't answer. If I tell him, he won't believe me. I can't explain how the Way Out signs turn to No Entry as I approach, how the escalators lead only to tunnels and stairs and back down to another platform, how the barriers come down and exits become solid walls. Time and time and time I've tried to follow the commuters, to mix in with them, to slip through unnoticed, but it never

works. I'm trapped. Doomed to ride the Circle Line. If I switch to the Northern Line or the Central or the District, no train ever comes. I can change platforms, change direction, but never leave. For fifteen years the world has passed me by in newspaper headlines: *Labour Victory, War in the Gulf, Millennium Dome.* None of it means anything to me. The world above might as well be another solar system for all I know of it. Sometimes I get a glimpse, when the train comes above ground at South Kensington or Tower Hill. But then the tunnels swallow me up again, and won't spit me out.

Runner's looking at me doubtful, at the ripped sleeve of my anorak, at my scuffed shoes. 'Hey,' he goes, 'you're not a—?'

I huff a laugh. No, I'm not a— Ghost, he means. But ghosts don't get hungry or scrabble for coins or need to pee.

'I might as well be,' I tell him.

'I've run away from home,' he confesses, as if I can't tell. 'Is that what you did?'

'Yeah. Ran away, fifteen years ago. Came to London to live rough. So here I am. Still here.'

'But you're not—' He screws up his face—maths not his strong point. He gets there in the end: 'twenty-seven!' He's staring at my face, looking for traces of the fifteen Circle Line years. 'You're only about the same age as me.'

I say nothing. Already told him.

And then I look at our two reflections in the black window opposite, two of us, side by side, and I start to think—what if he's staying down here, too? I could do with a friend. I can lead him in the Circle Game for ever—round and round, up and down, never finding a way out. Two of us. Scrabbling for coins, laughing at the passengers, sharing chocolate and chewing-gum.

So I don't know what makes me do it, but when the train judders to a stop at Embankment, I say to him, quick: 'Get out, kid. Now. While you can. Go *on!*'

He looks at me, his face pale and scared. He hesitates. Then he grabs his rucksack and sprints out.

'*Don't look back!*' I shout after him.

Am I saving him, or is he saving me? If he can get out, maybe he can take me with him. I follow, light-footed, almost tiptoeing. He follows the signs for *Way Out* and *Charing Cross*. Up the steps. I follow, a good way behind. There's no escalator here but I feel like I'm riding up on one, carried by the gliding steps. I try to breathe, dizzy with the smell of freedom, thinking of streets, people, parks, beyond the exit.

He gets to the top. His ticket's in his hand. He feeds it into the turnstile slot, and pushes through.

Then he looks back.

'*No!*' I shout.

Too late. I'm whirled into sick, black dizziness. When I open my eyes, there's no turnstile, no exit, no Runner—only a blank wall, and an arrow pointing back the way I've come. *Circle Line Only*. There's only one way to go. Down. Back down.

The Westbound platform's deserted. I wait by the tunnel entrance. I hear the underground rumble of a train approaching Eastbound, and footsteps of people getting off. This side, there's nothing. I stare into blackness, watching a sweet paper gust along the track. This is the loneliest place on Earth.

Fifteen more years of the Circle Game, and maybe I'll get another chance.

Danny's Last Duchess

DENNIS HAMLEY

1955. The British Railways Modernization Plan was announced. The unthinkable was going to happen. Steam was doomed.

And today they were off for a day's gricing at Rugby Midland: Danny, Fred, Boris, and Yakker. And Linda.

'Girls don't go train-spotting,' said Yakker.

'She's not,' said Boris. 'She's Danny-spotting.'

'Shut up,' said Danny. He was fed up with the scrawls on walls round the school and in the village:

L B

L

D S

TRUE

He hadn't asked for this. He got very angry when he was teased about it by kids he thought were his friends.

'She does, she *likes* you,' Fred once said. 'Sheila Samways said she'd told her to ask me to tell you.'

And Fred hadn't been alone. Every girl in their class claimed that Linda had asked her to ask someone to tell him. And it *irked* him, it really *irked* him. Especially when he had railways to think about.

Railways were what he thought about nearly all the time. Especially 'Duchesses'. Those great, massive, beautiful, powerful, fast Pacific 4-6-2 locomotives, the masterpiece of their designer, Sir William Stanier, FRS, after whom the last to be built was named. But Danny wasn't interested in the last to be built. What he worried about was the last still to be seen by him. 46227 *Duchess of Devonshire*. He always seemed to miss her. He'd waited at Watford for her when he was staying with one set of grandparents and Crewe when he was with another. He'd hoped she would roll into Glasgow Central with 'The Royal Scot' when he was with his Scottish auntie, or bring 'The Mancunian' into London Road when he was with his Manchester uncle. Never. 'She went through on the "Lakes Express" just before you got here,' they said. Or, 'If you'd waited another half hour you'd have seen her on "The Irish Mail".' The engine ran through his dreams, her half-hidden nameplate and dimly seen number taunting him, hauling huge expresses into the sky. If he ever copped *Duchess of Devonshire*, he sometimes thought, the world would end at once with a great explosion.

But it wasn't just Duchesses or merely copping more and more numbers in his Ian Allan British Railways stockbook before steam disappeared, like Boris, Fred, and Yakker. No, he cared about railways more than that. He read all he could find about them. He knew how they worked: he knew their history. And he tried to tell everybody. But they always shut him up.

The boys went to Rugby on the bus. That seemed a
bit silly, but the branch line serving their town ran the
other way. Just as they climbed in, Linda ran round
the corner, jumped on as well, followed them upstairs,
and sat on her own just behind them.

'What are you doing here?' demanded Fred.

'Mind your own business,' said Linda.

'You can't come train-spotting with us,' said Yakker.

'It's a free country,' said Linda.

Boris thumped Danny on the shoulder. 'She's after
you, she's after you,' he shouted.

'Shut up,' said Danny.

For the rest of the journey he sat unmoving, eyes to
the front, not saying a word except 'Shut up' now and
again while they teased him. All the way to Rugby.
Except once. As they neared Rugby, the road crossed
over the main line south of Rugby Midland station. A
northbound express went underneath, slowing for the
Rugby stop. Danny could see the engine was a Duchess,
but he couldn't make out the name or number. 'Did you
get it?' said Yakker. If one saw it, the rest felt they could
claim it. Except Danny. He wouldn't cheat.

'No,' said Boris.

'Wrong angle up here,' said Fred.

I bet it was *Duchess of Devonshire*, Danny groaned
inside his head.

'What's that?' Linda said suddenly.

She was pointing along the railway to a huge set of
criss-cross steel girders laid across it.

'It's a bridge,' said Boris contemptuously.

'I can see that. I'm not quite stupid,' said Linda.
'What's it for?'

Danny felt he had to tell her. 'It carries the line to
Sheffield and Manchester through Leicester Central
and Nottingham Victoria,' he said. 'The old Great

Central. The other Rugby station, Central, is just down
the line. They call the bridge the Birdcage. There's a
story about when it was built. You see, the . . . '

'Here he goes again,' said Yakker.

'Put a sock in it, Danny,' said Fred.

So he did, and stayed quiet for the rest of the day as
they crossed from platform to platform on the huge,
echoing Midland station. He copped a Princess Royal, a
couple of Rebuilt Scots, three Jubilees, ten Stanier
class 5's, six 8F's, four ancient wheezing Midland
Compounds, and three 2-6-0 'Crabs'. Four Duchesses
came through but his target wasn't one of them. As far
as copping new engines went it was good. But he was
haunted by the thought that he might have seen *Duchess
of Devonshire* that morning and not recognized her.

Linda had done nothing but hang around watching.
Sometimes she asked a question. No one answered.
Sometimes she said things like, 'Look, there's a nice
train coming in. It's all clean and shiny.' The boys
turned their eyes towards the all-over station roof and
wearily shook their heads.

'She's a blight,' said Boris.

'A pain,' said Fred.

'Just get rid of your girlfriend,' said Yakker.

'She's not my girlfriend,' said Danny.

It was mid-afternoon. The station was, for a little
while, quiet. Danny found himself looking at Linda.
Yes, he thought, really, she looks nice. She was small
and trim, her brown hair was tied in a ponytail and she
had laughing eyes. Perhaps . . .

'Get rid of her, I said,' Yakker repeated.

'How can I?' said Danny.

'I don't care. Just do it,' said Yakker.

Danny lumbered towards her.

'You'll have to catch me first,' shouted Linda.

Danny put out an arm to stop her. She ducked underneath, ran up the steps to the overbridge, down again to Platform 1, through the concourse and booking hall and into the road outside.

'Let her go,' shouted Boris. His voice echoed across the station. 'Then she'll have to go home on her own. That'll teach her.'

But Danny knew what it would be like if they went back without her. Linda's mother would be furious and indignant, the boys' mothers furious and embarrassed. As for the fathers . . . He hesitated a fraction, then he was off, pushing his way past surprised waiting passengers.

When he was outside the station he stopped. Where had she gone? If she'd run into the town he'd never find her. No, there she was, to his left, disappearing up an alleyway. He was off again.

The alleyway soon degenerated into a cindery path behind back gardens. Linda was ahead, still running.

On he pounded. In front he saw the embankment which carried the old Great Central to Leicester, Nottingham, and Sheffield. Proudly to his left stood the huge steel girders of the Birdcage. The path turned right and skirted the foot of the embankment, separated by a wooden fence.

Linda reached the turn. But she didn't follow the path. She stopped, turned towards him, and laughed. Then she climbed nimbly over the fence and started clambering up the embankment.

'Come back,' Danny shouted. 'You can't do that.'

'Who says so?' she answered.

'Everyone. It's trespassing.'

'That's never stopped you before.'

Well, no, it hadn't. But that was on the branch line at home, with only two trains a day. These were main

lines with huge expresses thundering by. She reached
the top and stood looking down on him. Of course, he
had to follow. He struggled up the steep embankment
through short, rough grass, reached the top and the
granite chips the track was laid in crunched under his
feet.

Where was she now?

He could hear her laughing. This was like chasing a
will-o'-the-wisp. Then he saw her, peeping out from
behind a girder on the Birdcage.

If I go near her, he thought, she'll start running
again and I'll never catch her. 'Stay there,' he shouted.
Vain hope.

'All right,' she answered unexpectedly.

Danny suddenly realized he was exhausted. He
trudged through the heavy granite ballast, expecting
her to dodge away again. But she didn't. She stood
there, waiting for him.

'You see?' she said. 'Why can't you trust me to
know best?'

'Why have you come up here?' he said wearily.

'I heard you say there was a story about when this
bridge was built and the others shut you up. I want to
hear it. So tell it to me.'

'You won't be interested,' Danny answered.

'Yes, I will. Honest.'

'All right,' he said. 'If you really want to know. That
line down there'—he pointed to the four running lines
and the fan of pointwork and sidings which led to Rugby
Midland—'was the first main line built out of London
to the north. The London and Birmingham Railway, it
was called. It became the London and North Western
afterwards. This line we're on now'—he indicated the
two running lines across the Birdcage that they were
standing on—'was the last. The Great Central out of

Marylebone up to Sheffield and Manchester. Well, the London and North Western wasn't too pleased about a new line coming to Manchester one way and London the other when that's what they had already. They thought they'd lose money. So when the Great Central wanted to build a bridge over their lines, they were furious. They tried to stop them, but they couldn't. So they made it difficult for them.'

'How?' asked Linda.

Danny looked at her. There wasn't a flicker of a smile on her face. If he hadn't known she couldn't be, he'd have thought she was hanging on to every word he said.

'Do you see those signals down below?' he said. He pointed to a huge signal gantry which spanned all the lines outside Rugby Midland.

Linda looked down. 'Yes,' she said.

'Do you notice anything strange about them?'

She peered at them for some seconds. 'There's a lot of them,' she answered at last.

Indeed there were. The tall posts were covered with semaphore signal arms with green and red shades at the rear end, like exotic fruit growing in a weird tropical forest.

Even as she watched, a high signal arm jerked upwards.

'There's a train coming,' said Danny.

'There must be two trains,' Linda answered. 'The arm underneath on the same post has gone up as well.'

'Ah,' Danny said triumphantly. 'That's the whole point. The two signals are the same. The top ones are just repeaters.'

'What a waste,' said Linda. 'Isn't one enough?'

'It should be,' said Danny. 'But when the London and North Western saw the Great Central building this massive great bridge, they said the steel girders would

get in the way of their signals so the drivers couldn't
see them. So they made the Great Central pay to make
the posts higher and put more signal arms on top, to
stand out against the sky above the bridge.'

'And do they?'

'Do they what?'

'Get in the way.'

'I don't know. I've never looked.' As an afterthought,
he said, 'They call this gantry the bedstead.'

Linda laughed. 'Birdcage and bedstead,' she said.

The train signalled below chuffed past. 'Stanier 2-6-4
tank,' said Danny. He consulted his Ian Allan book.
'Got it already.' They watched the engine drag its six
coaches out of Rugby. 'Just a local to Bletchley and
Northampton.'

'I liked that story,' said Linda.

Danny stared at her. 'You're having me on,' he said.

'No, really, I did. It was interesting. Especially the
way you told it.'

Danny looked at her. She really seemed to mean it.

The rails behind them were quivering and hissing as
if they had a life of their own.

'Something's coming,' said Danny. 'It's just leaving
Rugby Central.'

They heard the deep barks of a large engine restarting
a heavy load.

'Keep in,' said Danny. 'Stay close to the girders.'

The train drew near. They saw white steam from the
engine's cylinders and grey smoke from its chimney.
The noise grew deafening.

'Look,' cried Danny in delight. 'It's "The South
Yorkshireman". Marylebone, Sheffield, and Bradford.'
The headboard on the smokebox proudly proclaimed
the legend. 'It's an A3. A Gresley Flying Scotsman
class.' He saw the number on the smokebox door.

'60052,' he yelled. 'I don't think I've copped it.' In truth, he hadn't copped many Eastern engines. The massive locomotive drew level. The noise was tremendous. Linda put her hands over her ears. Danny wanted to, but wouldn't on principle. The two bogie wheels clanked past, then a blast of warm steam from the pistons, then the huge driving wheels turning not three feet away. Their wheelbeats on the bridge sounded like thunderclaps and the connecting rods on the complicated valve gear turned dizzyingly. Danny looked at the name on the splasher over the middle driving wheel. '*Prince Palatine*,' he shouted. The tender passed, then eight coaches. 'They're real Gresley coaches. None of your standard rubbish.'

The wheelbeats changed from thunder to sharp gun fire as the carriage wheels bit the rail joints. After what seemed an age of imprisonment, the last coach banged past. Danny turned through his Ian Allan book, found the class list and ticked *Prince Palatine* off.

'I never expected that cop today,' he said. 'All I want now is . . . '

'What does it mean when things are "gresley"?' Linda interrupted.

'Sir Nigel Gresley. Great man. He designed the engines on the old London and North Eastern Railway, and the coaches too.'

Linda was silent. So was the rest of the world now 'The South Yorkshireman' had passed. Then she said, 'Another signal on the bedstead has gone up.'

'It's over the southbound, fast line,' said Danny. 'Something big's coming through to London.'

He waited. The air was full of a strange expectancy. Far off he heard a deep carrying whistle and the steady chatter of a steam engine working fast. 'It's not stopping,' he said. 'It's running through.'

Suddenly he felt a hand searching out his. Linda had moved tight up to him. She took his hand before he could pull it away and squeezed it. Then she stood on tiptoe and lightly kissed him on the lips. He stared at her, amazed. She was smiling and her eyes were sparkling.

'There,' she said. 'That's better than any smutty old train, isn't it?'

He couldn't say a word. He just kept looking at her.

'Isn't it?' she asked again.

The roar below had grown until it was nearly deafening and even the Birdcage bridge seemed to shake. He tore his eyes away from Linda to look down. A huge Stanier Pacific in British Railways green hurtled underneath. There was a tartan-painted headboard on its smokebox: THE ROYAL HIGHLANDER. It hauled a long line of gleaming new maroon coaches with tartan destination boards: LONDON (EUSTON) – PERTH. But that engine: yes, it was a Duchess and—yes it was, *it was*, IT WAS—'46227 *Duchess of Devonshire*,' he shouted. '*I've got it, I've got it, I've got it.*' He danced on the granite ballast. And Linda danced with him.

The great express roared underneath on its way south. They were swathed in warm steam and smoke full of the unmistakable smell of a steam engine. In the fog he tried to open his Ian Allan book to note this greatest cop of all. But he couldn't: Linda was still holding his hand. He remembered that she'd asked a question and he hadn't answered it yet. The steam and smoke cleared. He could see her again. He looked at her as if for the very first time.

'Well, nearly,' he said.

Acknowledgements

David Belbin: 'Mystery Train', copyright © David Belbin 2001, first published in this collection by permission of Jennifer Luithlen on behalf of the author.

Ruskin Bond: 'The Tunnel' from *Time Stops at Shamli* (Penguin Books, India, 1989), first magazine publication in imprint (Bombay, 1976), reprinted by permission of the author. A similar version was published in *The Road to the Bazaar* (Julia Macrae, 1981).

Marjorie Darke: 'Corder's Spur', copyright © Marjorie Darke 2001, first published in this collection by permission of the author c/o Rogers Coleridge and White Ltd.

Robert Dawson: 'Grease Monkey Jack—the Engineer', copyright © Robert Dawson 2001, first published in this collection by permission of Laurence Pollinger Ltd on behalf of the author.

Adèle Geras: 'First Class', copyright © Adèle Geras 2001, first published in this collection by permission of Laura Cecil on behalf of the author.

John Gordon: 'Dust', copyright © John Gordon 2001, first published in this collection by permission of A. P. Watt on behalf of the author.

Dennis Hamley: 'Danny's Last Duchess', copyright © Dennis Hamley 2001, first published in this collection by permission of the author.

Douglas Hill: 'Train of Ghosts', copyright © Douglas Hill 2001, first published in this collection by permission of Watson, Little Ltd on behalf of the author.

Hilary McKay: 'Penalty for Improper Use', copyright © Hilary McKay 2001, first published in this collection by permission of Jennifer Luithlen on behalf of the author.

William Mayne: 'A Puff of Steam' from *Salt River Times* (Thomas Nelson Pty, 1980/Hamish Hamilton 1980), copyright © Mayne and Mayne Pty Ltd 1980, reprinted by permission of David Higham Associates.

Linda Newbery: 'The Circle Game', copyright © Linda Newbery 2001, first published in this collection by permission of A. P. Watt on behalf of the author.

Alison Prince: 'Cabbage Soup', copyright © Alison Prince